THE FRINGE SERIES

"Best science fiction I have read in a long while."
    ~Michael D. Griffiths, *SF Reader*

Fringe Runner is epic fun with great characters, action, and suspense. Rachel Aukes is the next big name in the Space Opera genre!"
    ~ Nicholas Sansbury Smith, best-selling author of the *Extinction Cycle* series

"A perfect read for fans of the fantasy and sci-fi genres."
    ~ Ethan Gregory, *One Guy's Guide to Good Reads*

"I would recommend this novel to anyone who likes action-filled space operas and stories about fighting against the ruling government."
    ~ *Audiobook Reviewer*

EARTH UNDER SIEGE

"...Everything I've come to expect from this author. It's packed full of action, drama, surprise and suspense at every turn."
    ~Silvia at *Goodreads*

"Highly Recommended. Five Mysterious Stars."
    ~*RBS Productions*

"A top ten book!"
    ~ *Step into Fiction*

THE DEADLAND SAGA

Included on Suspense Magazine's "Best of 2013" list

Listed by the Huffington Post as one of the Best Zombie Books

"100 Days in Deadland is a stunning exploration of the human spirit: survival and greed, good and evil...a microcosm of today's society wrapped up in a dystopian novel. Rachel Aukes has written a modern take on a classic. I for one, cannot wait for her next book."
    ~ *Suspense Magazine*

"Another great zombie survival book made its way to our hungry brains! The book never slows down, the events are unpredictable and the characters are well built.... So go get the book, you'll love this one!"
    ~ *Zombie-Guide Magazine*

"This book is 5 stars all the way. It is unlike any zombie or apocalyptic story I have ever read... *100 Days in Deadland* doesn't just tell a story about zombies, it tells a story about a person's struggle to survival in a world that has fallen apart and how that person grows and changes through it all."
    ~ *Horror Web*

"A great read about survival in an undead world."
    ~ *Buy Zombie*

FRINGE LEGACY

Waymaker Wars

Space Troopers

Flight of the Javelin

Bounty Hunter

Fringe Series

The Deadland Saga

FRINGE LEGACY

FRINGE SERIES
BOOK 5

RACHEL AUKES

WAYPOINT BOOKS

For Brian, always.

CONTENTS

CHAPTER 1

FOR THE FREE

First City, Alluvia

CORPS GENERAL BARRETT ANDERS stood in the underground chamber deep below the streets of First City. He was surrounded by a dozen faces—a few new to him, a few who were famous, and a few good friends. Before him rose the latest round of initiates, the only people in the assembly room not wearing hooded capes to conceal their faces. The war with the fringe had depleted the organization's ranks, which had led to Barrett learning of the Founders and being invited to become its new leader.

He took a breath and spoke loudly. "I, Mason of Alluvia, hereby induct you into the Secret Order of the Founders. Your role will be to help expand humankind across the galaxy. Do you accept?"

"I accept," the five initiates replied as one.

"Bare your arms," Barrett ordered. As they pulled off their shirts, he lifted a metal device resembling a giant chess piece. Beginning at the first initiate, he pressed the tip of the metal against the inner part of her bicep. The skin sizzled, and she sucked in a breath through clenched teeth. He continued on to the next initiate and the next, until he'd branded all five.

Before Barrett was invited to join, the Founders had three leaders. Of the three, only Seda Faulk still lived, but he'd broken away from the clandestine group to lead the fringe rebellion. The war had splintered the Founders, and the group had nearly dissolved. But enough members remained, and they knew the group needed to evolve if it was to continue to make a difference, let alone survive.

Barrett's predecessor, Gabriel Heid, had been shortsighted. Heid had believed the Collective was strongest when ruling the colonies with an iron fist. Heid had treated the colonies like children, failing to understand that they'd grown up and needed to go out on their own to thrive. Barrett and the rest of the members in the chamber believed that freedom—not limitation—strengthened humankind.

Whereas the Founders had once focused on controlling the Collective, they now had a new vision: Allow the Collective and the Alliance to manage themselves, and form a third entity focused on establishing new colonies.

As Corps General of the Collective Unified Forces, he led the military forces of both Alluvia and Myr. With the support of the Founders, he would take control of a significant portion of the CUF armada, morphing it from a peacekeeping force into an exploratory force. But the colonization fleet would be essentially dead in space without fuel from Terra, rilon from Playa, blue tea from Spate, and food from Darios...four colonies none too keen on working with anyone associated with the Collective.

It fell on Barrett's shoulders to win them over.

CHAPTER 2

HOUSE POLITICS

Tulan Port, Playa

ARAMIS REYNE LET the ice-cold winds blast him for a long second before hustling back inside and closing the door. He shivered but felt invigorated.

Jeyde Sixx looked up from the chair in which he was comfortably reclined. His brown eyes twinkled. "I can never figure out why you want to live here. This is exactly what I envision hell frozen over would look like."

He smiled. "It's not so bad. The air's crisp, there's no pollution, and the lower gravity can add a whole new level to sporting events."

Sixx nodded toward the door. "Crisp? Out there feels damn near as frigid as Mary, the Myrad madam."

Motion twenty feet behind Sixx drew Reyne's attention. It wasn't the construction crews working on the tunnel's walls. Their movements had become a part of the background over the past several weeks. It was the pair walking toward them in tailored clothes draped over their gravity suits. Only citizens wore clothes that nice.

He turned back to Sixx. "The thing I've always liked best about Playa is that it's the farthest world from Alluvia and Myr. In the past, the distance helped keep the citizens away."

Sixx turned to look. He pushed off the chair and to his feet, moving to stand protectively near Reyne's side. He was as tall as Reyne, thirty years younger, and well-built; a formidable defensive force. "Looks like they aren't wasting any time getting their claws into the new fringe station."

Reyne sighed. "Not when there's a chance for someone to get rich off someone else's hard work." He glanced at Sixx. "Make sure the dock operators notify us of all landings, especially Collective ships."

"You got it, boss."

The men watched the man and woman approach. Neither had bluish skin, indicating they were from Alluvia, which meant they'd at least be *slightly* easier to work with than the ever-snobbish Myrads. Reyne had even become friends with a few Alluvians over the years. Boden, when he wasn't on a Sweet Soy binge, made a damn fine mechanic on the *Gryphon* crew. Then there was Boden's pal, Kason, who'd found Reyne plenty of jobs when they still operated as runners.

Most citizens didn't like interplanetary mingling. Kason had been killed because of his association with colonists. Just like Gabriela Heid, who'd sacrificed everything to fight for the colonies' independence. As for the two approaching citizens, he suspected they were like all the other citizens he most certainly didn't like. Even though the colonies had broken free from the Collective to form the Alliance of Free Colonies, many citizens continued to act as though colonists existed to work for them.

Being a citizen used to mean having more rights than a colonist. Now, being a citizen simply meant someone was from

Alluvia or Myr, the only two planets remaining in the Collective. When the Alliance was formed, its members quickly chose to keep the title of "colonist" as a source of pride.

On Playa, the planet farthest from anything and anyone, the only citizens Reyne had ever seen on its surface were trying to either get rich off it or destroy it. With the newcomers' expensive-looking clothes, this pair was after the former.

They came to a stop before Reyne. Both looked to be in their thirties, but with the medical benefits the Collective provided its citizens, each could be anywhere from thirty to seventy. Their skin was paler than Reyne's dark skin. The woman was attractive except for an overly rigid posture, like tension from a life spent looking prim and proper had fused her bones together. The man moved smoothly, but his gaze bore a hawkishness that reminded Reyne of a ship mechanic who'd once tried to triple-charge him for an engine overhaul. He didn't like this man already.

Reyne told himself that, as Playa's only stationmaster, working with citizens was necessary. It didn't mean he had to enjoy it. "I didn't expect to see Collective representatives here for at least another week."

"As we're responsible for establishing the Collective properties at the docks and in the stationhouse, we wanted to be here as quickly as possible." The woman's words came out softer than he'd anticipated. She smiled. "Stationmaster Reyne, I've been looking forward to meeting you. I'm Hadley Goldsberry and this Simon Tate. As you've already surmised, we're representatives of Legacy Starporation, and will be your primary contacts with the Collective here at Playa Station. Simon is overseeing the construction of the Collective concourse at the docks, while I'm overseeing the construction of the Collective wing here in the stationhouse."

"Tulan Port," Reyne corrected.

"Pardon?" Hadley asked.

"Playa Station was just a working title until the Playans voted on its name. They chose to call it Tulan Port, since it's being built between where Ice Port and Tulan Base stood."

Her brow furrowed. "They named it after two colonies that were destroyed by bombings? That seems rather...dark."

"They chose the name to remember the families and friends they'd lost in the fight to win their freedom," Reyne corrected.

Simon rolled his eyes. "Those you talk of were insurgents responsible for murdering innocent citizens."

Sixx snorted behind Reyne, but didn't speak. Yep, Reyne did not like that man.

"Ah, so you're Jeyde Sixx. The infamous thief," Simon said, turning his attention from Reyne to Sixx.

"Those thievery claims are completely substantiated," Sixx said with a wide grin.

"You have outstanding warrants for theft on every world." Simon took a deep breath. "You also have something of mine I intend to get back."

"And just what might that be?" Sixx asked.

A sneer filled Simon's face, but he didn't answer.

"Simon, please," Hadley said before turning back to Reyne and Sixx. "I'm sure there's been a misunderstanding."

"I'm sure that's all it is," Reyne said, though he knew differently. Sixx had been a professional thief for nearly his entire life. He'd made more than a few enemies over the years.

"I apologize for any tension," Hadley said. "I don't want to get off on a rough start. I meant what I said before: that I've been looking forward to meeting you. I've followed your exploits and respect your dedication to improving the welfare of colonists. While I may have been born on Alluvia, I've been fascinated with colonist affairs since before the Uprising."

She was closer to his age than he'd guessed. He admitted that he found her intriguing. She could've said those words to placate him, but he sensed honesty in her. Still, he reminded himself that she represented the Collective, which meant he had no interest in continuing the conversation. "It's nice to meet you both. But if you'll excuse me, I need to get back to work."

"I understand. We have plenty to do as well," she said. They turned to leave, but she paused. "I'm sure we'll talk often as the space docks and stationhouse are built. I'd love to have tea some-time with you to talk through my ideas."

He shrugged. "Sure. I think I can make that work."

She smiled and dipped her head. "I look forward to working with you."

Simon left without giving Reyne any acknowledgement.

Tension tightened Reyne's muscles. He shook his heads. "Citizens."

Sixx mused. "She doesn't seem that bad...for a citizen, I mean. And she clearly doesn't think you seem too bad."

Reyne chortled. "You think she's interested in me? A citizen going for a colonist? That'll be the day." He waved Sixx off. "Besides, I don't have time for that."

"Maybe you should make time for that. You could use some-thing to take your mind off things."

"You mean, take my mind off things like what you stole from Simon Tate?"

Sixx held up his hands in surrender. "I have no idea what he's talking about." When Reyne continued to look at him dubiously, he added, "I mean it. I've never seen or heard of him until today. I'm not saying I haven't stolen something from him, I'm just saying it's not ringing a bell."

Before Reyne could scold Sixx for bringing on another problem courtesy of his kleptomania, Reyne's wrist comm chimed. He read the message that ran across the screen and sighed. "Ah, damn it. A dock worker just broke his leg. I'd better get down there."

"*We'd* better get down there," Sixx corrected. "After all, it's my job to keep you alive."

Reyne chuckled. "The war's over. It's safe to say no one sees this old man as a risk anymore."

It was Sixx's turn to chuckle. "You keep telling yourself that, boss."

Reyne fastened his cold weather gear. "Fine. Let's go. You can check in on Boden at the *Gryphon* then."

Sixx frowned. "Why me? You're the captain."

"Because the last time I checked in on him, he chewed my head off for asking him why he had one of my engines taken apart into a hundred pieces."

Sixx winced. "I almost miss the days he was on the Sweet Soy."

"I don't," Reyne countered, remembering Boden as a drug addict, so desperate for his next fix he'd steal anything or hurt anyone.

"He's taking Throttle's leaving hard," Sixx said.

"We all are," Reyne said softly before he put on his facemask and stepped outside.

An hour later, Reyne and Sixx returned to the stationhouse.

"This damned place never gets any warmer," Sixx said as he broke ice off his gear.

"You done yet? You haven't stopped complaining since we left the docks."

"I'll stop once the tunnel's completed between the docks and stationhouse. When's that again?"

"Not soon enough." Reyne had to admit that even he, a life-long Playan, felt chilled. Even though the docks were less than a half kilometer away, that was farther than anyone could survive outside without proper gear. At any time of day, the wind speed was higher than the temperature. After dark, during the "dead hours," the winds became so intense as to blow anything weighing under a ton into the frozen abyss. There was a reason everyone on Playa lived below ground or within its mountains.

Building a colony from scratch was a lot of work, but it was far easier than trying to clean up the bombed-out colonies. Reyne had briefly considered building at Tulan Base, but the entire mountain had been flattened, ruling it out. And he didn't want to go near Ice Port. His childhood home was a ghost town, its thirty thousand residents entombed in its frozen tunnels for eternity.

Reyne tried not to think about the friends he'd lost at Ice Port. Instead, he headed straight to the stationmaster's office, which was just to the right of the stationhouse's main entrance. Sixx had cautioned Reyne against being too accessible, but Ice Port had never been a highly populated colony and he expected Tulan Port to be no different.

Before he reached the door, one of the construction managers hustled toward them. The woman was well over seven feet tall, and thin. She wasn't quite a stretch, but her grandchildren would likely be born with a stretch's fully-mutated genes. Generations of Playan genetic lines that had gone without wearing gravity suits could no longer survive on any planet with higher gravity.

"Stationmastah," she said, with a strong local accent, "we got big problem."

"What's the problem?" Reyne asked.

She pointed in the direction of the tunnel where the Collective wing was being built. "They got bots, an' we got dropped. They say they got no need for us no more."

"Show me," Reyne said, and she led the pair of men to the tunnel.

"What'd she say?" Sixx asked quietly at Reyne's side.

"Seems our new friend, Hadley, brought in her own robotic workforce and fired all the local workers."

"They's creepy bots," she added.

As they ventured through the rocky tunnel, Reyne saw soon enough that the manager's words rang with truth. Tiny arachnid-like robots were running electrical cabling along the walls. Flat, circular bots, covered in hairy feelers, seemed to zigzag across the floor as they weaved the electromagnetic wiring that would be used to generate artificial gravity. He looked up and jumped a step back when he saw more of the circular bots working on the ceiling.

"Those are damn creepy bots," Sixx said.

"Told you so," the manager replied.

Reyne sighed. "Tell your crew to go home for the day. I'll get your jobs back."

She patted his shoulder. "You good man, Stationmastah."

She strode off, leaving the men standing alone with the army of robots.

One bumped Sixx's foot and he kicked it, sending it skidding a good twenty feet. It skittered back to work without pause. "Want me to fry their circuits? Because I can do that."

"No." Reyne sighed. "Seems I'm having that tea with Hadley after all."

CHAPTER 3

DÉJÀ VU

SEDA FAULK WAS in the middle of negotiating a trade deal when Hari entered the room and zeroed in on him. "I'm sorry to interrupt, but I need to speak with you, Mr. President," she said, not sounding the least bit apologetic.

With a sudden sense of unease, he stood. He turned to the citizens and colonists sitting on opposite sides of the large conference table. "Please continue. I'll return shortly."

He followed Hari out of the room. "What is it?" he asked as soon as the door closed behind them.

"You'll never believe it," she said as she rushed him down the hallway, "but a call has just come through *the* tablet."

He frowned. She spoke of his Founders tablet, a device he hadn't used since Mason pulled a coup, killed Seda's wife, and tried to have him killed. The Founders who'd broken off the larger group and joined the fringe, like Hari and Seda, knew better than to use the tablet for communications. When they broke away from the organization, they no longer considered themselves Founders. Seda had even considered destroying the tablet on more than one occasion. "Who's the caller?"

She looked around before answering in a hushed tone. *"Mason."*

Seda came to a stop. "That's impossible."

She tugged him forward. "I know."

They entered his office and closed and locked the door. Hari lifted the tablet she'd been hiding within her jacket and handed it to him.

He entered his passcode, and the screen came to life. While the account was Mason's, Gabriel Heid's was certainly not the visage that appeared on the screen. Seda's eyes narrowed. "Corps General, what game are you playing?"

"No game," Anders replied. "I have a question for you. I believe that once you're a Founder, you're always a Founder. Do you agree with that statement, Seda, or should I say, Aeronaut?"

Seda thought for a long moment before answering. "I agree...Mason."

Anders nodded, then smiled. "Good. Then I have a tremendous opportunity for you."

CHAPTER 4

BUG INFESTATION

Tulan Port, Playa

HADLEY CAME to Reyne's office, since hers was still being dug out from Playa's thick bedrock. She'd changed into a more casual tunic with feminine flowing pants. She walked less stiffly, or perhaps, because her hair was down, she seemed more approachable.

He motioned toward the couches off to the side of his office. "Have a seat, Citizen Goldsberry."

"Please, call me Hadley."

"Then you can call me Aramis. Or Reyne, or whatever suits your fancy."

"Aramis it is, then." When she sat, her smile morphed into a frown as she tried to smooth the fabric over the barely visible gravity suit she wore underneath her outfit. "It will be so nice when we finally have full gravity throughout the stationhouse. These suits are rather chafing."

"We expect to have it in the main tunnels and offices within the week; at least, the ones that have been built," he said. "Not having full gravity speeds up the heavy construction work, so you'll see it turned off every now and then as we build out the tunnels."

"I shouldn't complain," she said. "Lower gravity has its perks. My hair has never had as much body as it does here."

"It looks nice. I meant to say, you look nice," Reyne said sincerely.

Her smile grew. "Why, Aramis, I never took you for the complimentary type."

"I've been known to hand out a compliment or two." He strode over to the bar. "I had to do some digging around to find some tea around here, but I can't say I've ever had tea before."

"No, I don't suppose you have. I pictured you more as a whiskey man."

"Brandy is my preference," he said. "But whiskey has a nice burn to it."

He picked up the two cups he'd prepared and handed one to her before taking a seat on the opposite couch.

She took a drink, then winced slightly.

"Not a fan of the tea?" Reyne asked.

"It's a tad bitter, but not bad. How long did you let it steep?" she asked, and took another drink, this time without wincing.

"I don't know, maybe a half hour or so."

Her lips curled upward. "That explains it then."

He shrugged. "Tea has to be imported, and they typically send the crap out here. Playa's underground gardens are restricted to growing only the essentials for survival, and tea's never been considered an essential."

Hadley chuckled. "My mother would disagree. She loves her tea so much that she bought a tea boutique in First City." She paused. "But you don't have any interest in learning about me."

"You're wrong. I wouldn't mind getting to know you."

"Really?"

Reyne stammered. "Sure, in a work capacity, of course."

"Of course." She inhaled. "So, what's on your mind—in a work capacity?"

Reyne put his mug down. "Well, the local workforce, for starters. Playa's not an easy place to live. As I'm sure you've already noticed, credits don't exactly flow out this far in the fringe. That's why we help each other out whenever we can around here. That crew you let go today? They needed those jobs to put food on the table."

"I understand, but I receive direction from my superiors at Legacy Star. They sent the bots with Simon and me, and they expect them to be used." She shrugged. "And from a budgetary standpoint, the bots are a godsend. They work nonstop for minimal maintenance costs. With them, I can finish the wing two months faster and at nearly half the cost than if I pull from the Playan workforce."

"I understand, but we're talking about people's livelihoods here. If you crap on them now, what do you think is going to happen when you no longer have the bots and you need to hire staff to maintain your wing or whatever else you've been brought here to do?"

"A resort," she said. "That's my dream, anyway. I took the stationhouse job in exchange for managing the resort. I plan to draw in tourists. Tourism brings jobs and money."

Reyne laughed. "Tourists don't want to vacation on an ice world."

Her chin jutted upward. "They will if we can give them a serene winter wonderland. And the faster I can get a resort up and running, the sooner Playans prosper."

He shook his head. "Playans may find service jobs at your grand resort, but they won't prosper. Whoever owns the resort is who'll get rich."

She frowned. "There are many good careers involved in running a resort."

"And how many of those jobs will go to Playans?" Reyne asked.

"Over eighty percent," she countered. "But you're focused on the small picture. Tourism brings in people spending money at local businesses. Tourism is good for everyone in the area."

His eyes narrowed. "Tourism is good for the area if tourists actually leave the resort. With the weather around here, I'm guessing your resort is going to be all-inclusive."

"It has to be. We can't have tourists walking around outside and freezing to death." She sighed. "I really do want to see Tulan Port thrive. I plan to make my home here, but my hands are tied. If Legacy Star doesn't think I'm working in their best interests, they'll replace me. I worked my entire life for an opportunity like this. I need this job."

They sat in silence for a length.

Reyne considered their options. "I think we can find a solution that both includes local crews and meets your bosses' expectations so that you keep your job." He tacked on with a grin, "After all, I much prefer your company to Simon's."

"Oh, you'll still get to work with Simon plenty at the docks." She sobered. "His best friend was killed a year or so back and it changed him. And not for the better." Her smile returned. "On the bright side, I believe Simon plans to return to Alluvia as soon as the Collective concourse is fully operational."

"Then we'd better make sure his project finishes on time."

"We've found something we agree on," she said with a grin.

"It's a start. I'll take it," Reyne said. "As for our current dilemma, I think we can help each other out in ways that don't break your budget."

"How so?"

"I've seen your drilling bots. They're inefficient. I have

drilling machines and crews that have some scheduled downtime. I can see that you have access to them to drill out the remainder of your wing. A few hours with a drill team will cut days off your schedule."

"That may work," she mused. "But the budget will be tight."

"We'll figure it out," he said. "This isn't space. The Collective doesn't have to operate in a vacuum here."

Her lips curled upward. "I know. But now that the colonies are independent, everything's up in the air."

"We'll make it work. Together," Reyne said. He leaned forward. "So, does that mean the crews can return to work tomorrow?"

She gave a tight smile and nodded. "Yes. I can't speak for Simon at the docks, but yes, I give you my word that I'll leverage the Playan labor force here at the stationhouse. I'll look into ways to utilize the bots that won't replace human labor or put my time-line at risk."

"Good," he said. "I was hoping we could work together rather than against each other."

She smiled. "I hope for the same." She pushed to her feet. "Thank you for the tea."

He winced. "Oh, there's one more thing."

"What's that?"

"Business permits."

"Business permits? I don't understand."

"All business permits in Tulan Port must be approved by the stationmaster. That'd be me. But until you mentioned building a resort, I'd never heard a thing about it. And that sounds like a pretty big thing I should've heard about."

Her jaw slackened. "I didn't know."

"No problem. Get an application to me. Then we can bring in the number crunchers and start addressing the nonnegotiables, like how it's going to be a joint Legacy Star-Tulan Port project."

Her eyes widened. "Oh, Aramis. I don't think that will go over very well with my investors."

He shrugged. "Just tell them, 'Welcome to the Alliance of Free Colonies.'"

She cocked her head. "You underestimate the stubbornness of Legacy Star."

He smirked. "I bet we can make them come around."

She returned his smile. "You do make things interesting."

He walked her to the door. "Maybe next time we can take a break from talking about work stuff."

She touched his hand. "I'd like that very much."

He closed the door behind her and leaned against it, savoring her last words before heading back to his bar. He drank the brandy straight from the bottle. Hadley was decent enough, but why had he ever agreed to be the stationmaster? He hated politics and red tape, so what had he done? Found a bureaucratic job that ensured he spent days and nights behind a desk and talking work.

He needed to get Tulan Port up and running so he could retire, and perhaps even find time to enjoy a woman's company.

Taking the bottle to the desk, he sat and checked his messages. The tension in his shoulders dissipated when he saw one from Throttle. He ignored the other messages and opened hers.

Dad—

We hit a milestone! Jump fifty is done. We went beyond the Collective charts two weeks ago, so now we're running off our own scans, which means it takes longer between jumps to set up our next coordinates. I've attached our current scans in case you find yourself on a colony ship with a ton of juice.

The crew's getting along great. Our intrepid colonists

are another story. How can grown adults nitpick over the most trivial things? Today, it was the Spaten group accusing the Darions of keeping the good cavote spices to themselves. Yesterday, it was who got bathroom duties. I'm going to kill them! (Just kidding, I'm not going to kill them, even though Birk isn't convinced.) Anyway, I'll send you another message after our next jump. Hope you're staying warm on Playa (ha ha, like that's possible).

    —Throttle

Reyne's smile faded when he saw the timestamp. The message had been sent four days earlier. It'd been nearly a year since she left the fringe to fly into the unknown. The time lag grew as the distance between them increased, and his heartache deepened as Throttle flew farther away.

Flying a colony ship into the unknown was an unthinkable risk. Without charts, she could jump through an asteroid. Once the ship ran out of juice, it would be dependent on solar sails. By then, it would be a matter of chance of the ship finding a habitable world before the food on board ran out. Reyne tried not to think about the odds Throttle faced.

Instead, he typed out a reply, being careful to sound upbeat. She had enough to deal with. She didn't need the worries of an old man to add weight to her shoulders. Finished, he leaned back in his chair.

He read through her message again, trying to imagine what her days were like on board the *Gabriela*. Lost in his daydreams, he barely registered a metal-on-metal sound in the air vents.

He cocked his head and listened. Sure enough, the odd skittering sound came from the vents, and was growing louder. He walked over to the vent in the wall near the floor. He knelt to look inside, only to jump back when a small spider bot slammed into the metal screen covering the vent. It reversed, only to ram into the screen again, reversed, and kept repeating the process.

Reyne let his breath out. "Seems your programming got messed up, little guy, to get yourself stuck in the vents."

A second small bot joined the first, and the pair dented the screen. Reyne frowned. Then more bots arrived, all ramming against the screen, bowing it outward more and more with each approach.

Reyne reached for the photon gun on his thigh before realizing that he'd quit carrying it while working at the stationhouse, since Sixx was always at his side. But he'd sent his friend home early today because of his meeting with Hadley.

He spun on his feet and lunged to his desk. The bots broke out of the vent with a screech at the same time he opened the desk drawer and pulled out his gun. He yanked it from its holster, swung, and blasted away at the tidal wave of bots pouring from the vent and racing toward him. Each bot was only a few inches around, but there were so many that he wiped out several with each shot.

He kept firing nonstop at the bots nearest to him, but they were closing the distance. As he fired, he took steps back. They blocked off his escape route. He continued backpedaling until his heel bumped against a couch. The first bot reached him and leapt onto his leg. Its pincers, used for cutting and soldering wires, pierced Reyne's pants and his skin, sending a stab of fire through his thigh.

"Son of a—" he cried out and tumbled over the couch, using his gun to scrape the bot off him. He rolled to his feet as the bots climbed up the back of the couch and over. An idea struck him, and he continued to fire as he dove for the bar. He reached for the bottle of Terran whiskey Critch had given him and threw it at the approaching horde. The bottle shattered. Reyne fired at the bottle, and the high alcohol content in the liquor started a fire with a *whoomph*. The fire quickly spread to the couch, engulfing much of the bot army.

The fire alarms sounded, and Reyne was thankful that the fire suppression system wasn't scheduled to be installed for another two days.

He shielded his face from the heat while he shot the bots not caught in the fire. The air became harder to breathe, and he jogged around the spreading fire, in which the bots crackled like damp firewood in the flames. He reached for the door, and it opened to reveal a fire responder, who grabbed him and pulled him from the room.

"Is anyone else in there?" she asked.

Reyne went to answer but coughed. He shook his head.

She nodded, released him, and headed into the room, followed by several more responders carrying suppression tanks.

Reyne walked several steps to find fresher air to breathe, though nothing soothed his raw throat. Through his teary, burning eyes, he saw Sixx running toward him. Within seconds, Sixx grabbed Reyne's shoulder.

"You okay?" Sixx asked.

"Fi—" Reyne coughed.

Sixx noticed the gun still in Reyne's grip. He scowled, then shrugged. "Things were getting downright dull around here. I figured it was just a matter of time before someone would try to kill one of us."

CHAPTER 5

SCAVENGER HUNT

Devil Town, Spate

CRITCH LEFT his breather mask on as he walked through the sparse bar, even though the air inside was fine. The two drunks at the bar checked him out but returned to their drinks, unimpressed. The bartender kept an eye on him as he crossed the bar and headed straight for the stairs. He could still feel the bartender watching him as he climbed the stairs, though he knew he was doing nothing out of the ordinary aside from leaving his mask on.

Without the mask, everyone on Spate would recognize Critch's scarred face. Most of the fringe thanked him for their independence. Most of the Collective blamed him for a costly war and wanted him dead. He'd heard the price on his head had gone up since the war, which was surprising since that number had already been the highest in history.

He didn't take off the mask until he reached the top of the stairs. There, he found a petite woman—more of a girl than a woman—sprawled sideways in a chair, reading a tablet. She looked up and stared at him for a moment, and then her eyes widened. "You're Drake Fender."

Another woman stepped out of her room. When she noticed Critch, she grinned and rushed over to him. "Critch! Sweetie!"

Both women clung to him like leeches, albeit sexy and attractive leeches. Each murmured in his ear, telling him what she'd do to him should he buy her particular services. His brows raised. The younger woman must be incredibly flexible.

"Back off, girls. He's mine," a voluptuous brunette with a booming voice said as she approached Critch. The other two women promptly released him and stepped away.

"Been a long time, Lucy," he said to the madam.

"Too damn long." She wrapped herself around his waist.

He embraced her and kissed her cheek, brushing his lips closer to her ear. "I need some information," he whispered.

"Mm. Of course." She pulled back with a smile, took his hand, and led him down the hallway. Before they entered her room, she turned to the pair of women still in the hallway. "No one disturbs us, not for anything. Got it?"

She didn't wait for an answer before tugging Critch into her suite. As soon as they were inside, she released him, but not before patting his butt and giving him a wicked grin.

"Have a seat." She closed and then locked the door. She walked over to a table and poured two drinks.

Critch took a chair near the fireplace vid screen. "Why's the bar so empty?" he asked after accepting the glass of whiskey.

Lucy sat comfortably on the chaise in front of the window. "Business downstairs hasn't been so good since the war. Things in Devil Town are the best they've ever been. The CUF's no longer stealing half our income, so people are working longer hours by choice. There are more jobs than workers. But mostly, we no longer have to worry about our kids being taken away. Divorce rates are dropping, and people are spending more time at home. But they still come after their work shifts, more to socialize and celebrate than to drink away their sorrows."

"And business upstairs?"

A sensual smile curved her lips upward. "Better than ever. Bad times, good times, people always want to add a little spice to their lives. How's business treating you at Nova Colony?"

He took a drink. The whiskey was good, but it was no Terran whiskey. "Can't complain. I've left it in capable hands while I take a vacation."

She belted out a laugh. "In all the years I've known you, how many vacations have you taken?"

He shrugged.

"None," she answered for him. "And I'd lay a safe bet that you've never taken a vacation in your entire life. So, what brings you to Devil Town—wait, no, let me guess. You're looking for your ship?"

He eyed her. "What have you heard?"

She leaned back onto the chaise and propped her head on her hand. "I heard your good-for-nothing pilot ran off with your ship, leaving you stranded in the middle of a battlefield surrounded by the whole damn CUF army."

He gave a simple nod. "That sounds about right."

She continued. "I heard he used up all the ship's juice jumping from the armada as well as your specters. He ended up here on Devil Town, assuming we'd already beaten the CUF. He was wrong."

He swallowed. "What happened to my ship?"

"The CUF commander here was going to blow it up, but then the peace treaty happened, and we Spatens made sure every citizen hightailed it out of here posthaste. Those who didn't leave fast enough, well, let's just say they're no longer doing any kind of anything anymore." She grinned. "We accumulated a nice collection of cars and apartments that were abandoned. If you really want to have a bit of vacation, you and I can have some quiet time at my new place on Summers Place if you'd like."

He ignored her. "Where's the *Honorless* now?"

She waved him off. "At the impound lot. Most people know not to mess with your stuff, but I can't guarantee it's still in one piece."

He downed the whiskey, set the glass on the table, and stood.

"Don't you want to know about your pilot?" she asked.

"Where's Gabe?" he asked, baited.

"He got himself arrested for trying to skip out on paying what he owed. He's still down on Debtor's Row in case you'd like to pay him a visit."

Critch's lip curled upward. "I think I'll do that."

He looked down at his wrist comm and tapped out several commands. "There. That should cover our time together."

She glanced down at her wrist comm and smiled before looking back up. "Next time, don't wait so long before coming back for a visit."

He tilted his head in her direction. "You take care of yourself, Lucy," he said and let himself out.

He hustled down the stairs, donning his mask along the way. Several more patrons had arrived, and the bar had a life to it that it hadn't had earlier. A few tables were filled, and many of the barstools were now occupied. His step hitched when he noticed a patron at the bar who didn't quite fit in. For being alone, he didn't seem drunk, and he didn't watch the wall screens.

Critch continued through the bar, heading straight for the door. He stepped through the inner doorway and into the airlock chamber, opening the outer door as soon as the first door sealed shut. Once outside, he hustled down the sidewalk, making a sharp turn at the end of the block. There, he waited.

After a couple minutes, Critch resumed his walk, but he still couldn't shake the feeling that the man in the bar wasn't there for a drink. Critch's gut instincts had never steered him wrong, and they were currently telling him that he was being followed.

CHAPTER 6

COLLECTIVE GRIDLOCK

Parliament, Myr

CORPS GENERAL BARRETT ANDERS stood at the podium before Parliament. The last time he'd stood in that place, he'd been stripped of his command and they'd declared war on the colonies. While he knew they had far less power this time, he didn't set his expectations very high. Parliament had been ineffectual two years ago, and the news showed it'd only worsened since the colonies left the Collective.

"The Collective is failing," Anders began. "In the past year, the colonies have broken off to create the Alliance of Free Colonies. Our economy is the weakest it's been in over two hundred years. We're not failing because the colonies became independent. We're failing because we didn't plan for that inevitability. Even now, we're still focused on the colonies. You're spending all your debates and energies on how to use the colonies—through trade and negotiations—to make the Collective strong. You're searching for water in a dry creek bed."

Murmurs arose from the senators.

"And just what do you propose we do?" a senator yelled out.

Anders continued. "You need to quit clinging to the past and look outward to a sustainable future."

The discontent grew in volume.

Anders tamped down the air. "The Collective began with two planets. The two then grew into three, then four, and eventually to six planets. Now we've returned to two."

"Get to the point," someone yelled.

"We grew through colonization," Anders said. "There's nothing stopping us from colonizing once again."

"It's impossible!"

Anders scanned the crowd to see the senator who'd spoken now standing. "How so?"

"All the colonies are within our star system. To colonize into another system would take years and resources we don't have."

"Colonization missions would take years, yes," Anders said. "Longer now that nearly all fuel production facilities were destroyed in the war. But we have more than enough resources. We have many times the resources the first colonists had when they reached Alluvia. In fact, we have an entire *armada* of resources."

Senators laughed, yelled, and complained.

A senator slapped her microphone until the room quieted. "Corps General, are you proposing we give up the only thing we have that keeps the Alliance from seizing our lands and people?"

"I'm not proposing leaving the Collective without a peacekeeping force," Anders responded. "Although I believe you are making a rather large and misinformed assumption if you believe the colonies will turn around and do to us what we did to them."

More murmurs of discontent ensued.

"As its leader, I understand the capabilities of the Collective Unified Forces better than anyone else. The truth is, we have more ships than we have dromadiers to crew them. I propose the

CUF be split into two branches: the Collective Unified Forces, the peacekeeping force as we understand it today; and the Collective *Exploratory* Forces, for establishing colonies in new systems."

"That's ludicrous!" a senator shouted.

Anders cocked his head. "Really? Yet, the Alliance has already sent a colony ship beyond our system."

Complete silence fell over Parliament. He found some level of satisfaction at realizing they hadn't known.

"The Alliance of Free Colonies is looking at expanding their empire. If you don't look at expansion, then you'd better get comfortable with the idea that your children and your children's children will be part of a fading Collective and will one day beg to become a part of the Alliance." Anders took a deep breath. "I'm not asking you to make a decision today. I'm asking you to consider the proposal. Now, how many of you are open to discussing the Collective's expansion through new colonies?"

Only a few hands raised before a cacophony of complaints and disagreements erupted.

"You're too focused on maintaining your current standard of living rather than looking at what's needed for the future," Anders said, though he suspected none could hear his words above the bombardment. After watching the crowd of monkeys slinging shit before him, he scowled. "You're useless to me."

Another thing Parliament didn't yet know was that Anders had long since pulled all the strings he had across the armada to claim and quietly retrofit seventeen CUF ships for a long-term mission. He stepped down and strode from Parliament without a single glance over his shoulder.

CHAPTER 7
CHARRED RUMINATIONS

Tulan Port, Playa

REYNE KICKED a melted bot across the blackened floor. Around him, everything that'd been in his office was either ashes or charred clumps of debris. The stone walls, covered in soot, were otherwise fine. Durability of infrastructure was one of the few nice things about living in Playa's underground tunnels. A consistent temperature was another nice thing, but at the moment Reyne wasn't paying much attention to that.

Sixx tsked. "What a perfectly good waste of Terran whiskey."

Reyne rubbed a burn near his elbow. "Better it than me."

Boden did a three-sixty, taking in the room. He walked over to the vent, knelt, and examined it.

Bree picked up a scorched spider bot and juggled it in her hands. "I can't believe someone's trying to kill you."

"But I've been saying it all along," Sixx said.

She rolled her eyes at him. "Yeah, but you always think someone's out to kill us."

Sixx lifted his chin. "And have I ever been wrong?"

"You really want me to start a list?" she countered.

Boden returned and faced Reyne. "Are you sure the bots were sent to kill you? Maybe they were sent into your office to steal something, and you were there."

"Not a chance," Reyne said. "Those little bastards came right at me. They weren't acting erratic like wires got crossed somewhere. Those things were programmed to come into my office and kill me. You should've seen them. They were like tiny maniacal killers on eight legs."

Sixx cocked his head. "If these were the same bots we saw working the Collective wing, it narrows down our list of suspects. I haven't seen any other groups around here supplement their workforce with spider bots."

"Agreed," Reyne said. "I'd bet my life that these bots were Legacy Star bots, which means I need to talk with the two Collective representatives here in Tulan Port."

Sixx mused. "Simon? I could see that. Hadley? She seems too nice."

"Those are the ones to watch out for the most," Bree said.

Reyne frowned, neither liking the idea nor discounting it. "We have to assume it could be either or both of them, or anyone on their staff."

"It could be an attempt at a coup," Sixx said. "The best time for the Collective to take control of Tulan Port is before we have our defenses in place."

"Or, it could be someone trying to make it look like a citizen is trying to kill you," Bree said. "No one would think twice about a citizen doing something like that, so it'd be a perfect cover if it was a colonist."

"Why would a colonist try to kill Reyne?" Boden asked.

Bree shrugged.

"There are plenty of reasons," Sixx said. "Someone blames you because their kid died during the war, someone doesn't want you as a stationmaster, someone craves your job, someone simply doesn't like you—"

Reyne feigned disgruntlement. "Who wouldn't like me?"

Sixx eyed him. "Maybe it's not even personal. The war's over, but the Alliance is new. Maybe it's just someone trying to make a statement by taking out a stationmaster."

"That sounds very personal to me," Reyne said.

Bree sighed. "Instead of sitting around and talking about who tried to kill our friend, how about we start asking around to see if anyone saw or heard anything."

The crunching sound of burnt debris brought everyone's attention to the doorway to see Hadley step inside. She looked around, mouth open, while the others watched her with distrust. When she saw Reyne, she approached. "I came as soon as I heard there was a fire. What happened?"

"Seems some of your bots thought to pay me a visit after you left yesterday," Reyne said.

"What?" She shook her head. "I don't understand."

"He's saying your little spider bots tried to kill him right after you left him alone," Sixx answered, tossing a melted unit toward her.

She caught it and stared, seemingly genuinely confused. But Reyne no longer knew what to think about her. He'd liked her right off the bat, but her charisma could just as easily have been an act. He'd been a poor judge of character in the past. And had paid the price.

Her brow furrowed. "I don't know how they could do something like that. They're specifically programmed for simple, repeatable construction tasks."

"Maybe they're programmed for more than just construction," Sixx said.

"They are not preprogrammed to kill, if that's what you're trying to say," she snapped at him.

"Where are your bots now?" Reyne asked.

Hadley turned back to him. "Ten are with the crews, laying wire. I sent the rest to assist Simon at the docks this morning. All my bots were accounted for at that time. I can have them returned if you'd like to see them."

"No," Reyne said, not wanting to see one more of the creepy-crawlies ever again.

"Yes. Bring me one," Boden countered. "I want to go through its code."

"Of course, though I don't know if it will do you any good," she said.

Boden's features tightened as he thought. "Can you also provide us Legacy Star's shipping manifests that show how many bots were delivered to Tulan Port?"

"I'll run an inventory on all bots in operation. I'll get those numbers to you this morning." She noticed the burns on Reyne's arms, and her eyes widened as she rushed closer. "You're hurt! Are you okay?"

"Injuries sometimes happen when someone tries to kill you," Bree said drily.

Hadley ignored her. "I don't understand why someone would do this to you. Doesn't everyone understand that you're trying to make things better on Playa?"

"Obviously not everyone's a fan," Reyne said, taking a step back, not fully convinced that Hadley didn't know more than she was letting on.

She noticed the movement, and her lips thinned. "Well, please know that I do care, and I'll have the bot and numbers sent over right away. You know how to reach me."

She left the room.

"You know," Sixx began, "if she's not trying to kill you, you'll have some apologizing to do."

Reyne shrugged.

Bree scowled. "Hadley was the only person besides Sixx who knew you'd be alone here."

"Are you saying that I'm a suspect?" Sixx asked.

Bree thumped his shoulder. "Not this time, sugar. Hadley tops my list."

Sixx then turned to Boden. "You realize that any bot Hadley delivers will have been wiped clean. The same with any numbers she provides. There's no way she'd give us anything that might implicate her or her employer."

Boden shook his head. "There are always footprints left in bot programming. If she wipes it, I'll see it."

"And the numbers?" Sixx asked.

"If she's not lying, and I know that's a big *if*, I want to see if the bots that went after Reyne were listed on the manifest. If all the Legacy Star bots are accounted for, then we have to assume there could be many more out there."

Reyne winced. "You think there could be more murder bots scurrying around Tulan Port than the ones on the construction crews?" He shivered.

"That's just creepy," Sixx added.

A man stepped into the office. He wore the black jumpsuit of the construction crews. "'Scuse me, Stationmastah. We's starting on yo' office now. We's have it fixed within a day"

Reyne motioned him inside. "It's all yours."

Reyne, Sixx, Bree, and Boden left the office for the construction crews. On his way out, Reyne turned back to the Playan. "Oh, and when you replace the vent covers, be sure to use rilon."

The man frowned, then shrugged. "Sho' thing, Stationmastah."

Reyne joined his friends in the hall.

"Rilon will keep bots from coming through the vents," Boden said, "but we need to ramp up security on any access point to your office. I think your door should also be rilon, since we have plenty of it here on Playa."

"Just because we have plenty of it doesn't make it cheap," Reyne said. "But if it makes you feel better, I'm all for it."

Boden had always been a good mechanic. That attention to detail had flooded over into other aspects of his life since Throttle left. It was as though Boden kept his mind off her by trying to keep it busy all the time. Reyne had expected Boden to run back to the Sweet Soy. The Alluvian had surprised him and stayed clean, though Reyne wondered if that was more due to the fact that Sweet Soy was nearly impossible to find on Playa than anything else.

Boden nodded. "I'll give some thought to what else we can do. We have to fortify your office. Same with your apartment. When they come after you again, you might not be so lucky."

"Lucky?" Reyne guffawed. "It wasn't luck. I fought them off with pure skill...and maybe a touch of luck."

"Let's not count on luck next time," Sixx said. "We'll rotate shifts. Boden, Bree, and I will each take ten-hour shifts every standard day."

Reyne frowned. "I don't need to be babysat."

"If something happens to you, I'm out of a job," Sixx said. "Who's going to hire a thief with outstanding warrants on every planet?"

"Ex-thief," Bree corrected.

"Sure," Sixx said, not inspiring confidence in his changed ways.

"You?" Boden said. "How about me? No one in the Alliance will hire an Alluvian drug addict, and no one in the Collective will hire an expat citizen."

"I have you both beat," Bree said. "No one would hire me, since I'm listed as deceased on all records. Hard to hire a corpse."

Sixx turned back to Reyne. "See, boss? We're not babysitting you; we're looking out for our own well-being."

Reyne cocked his head. "Now I'm beginning to wonder if I shouldn't make my hiring requirements a bit stricter when taking on new crew members."

"Nah," Sixx said. "I think you've got them at just the right level."

Reyne sighed. "Okay, illustrious crew, let's go find ourselves an assassin."

CHAPTER 8

UNPAID DEBTS

Devil Town, Spate

DEVIL TOWN HAD BEEN BUILT on gambling and prostitution, so it was no surprise that Debtor's Row was the largest wing of Devil Town's prison. When tourists didn't return home, chances were they were either dead or locked up in Debtor's Row, which wasn't much better. There, debtors worked off their obligations through hard labor, mostly cutting through rock to enable Devil Town's expansion. Working outdoors day in and day out, wearing breather masks, would be hard on even the healthiest person. Add vigs to the mix—vicious rodents the size of swine—and every hour outdoors was dangerous.

Spate, for its sizable human population, was a desolate world with an atmosphere devoid of oxygen and carbon. Every building, including the massive city gardens, were sealed ecosystems. Outside the protective biospheres, Spate was as rocky as Terra but had nothing else in common with Critch's home world.

There was a reason the first colony on Spate was called Devil

Town. It drew in its victims with promises of pleasure, only to take their souls—and all their money.

A debtor had to work one year for every thousand credits owed, which meant many of the current inmates would die long before their debts were written off. The punishment was harsh, but living in a colony without air was harsh. Colonists had a hard enough time scraping by as it was, though Critch suspected the economies across the colonies would improve now that the Collective no longer played puppet master.

Devil Town's prison stood tall on the colony's outskirts. Critch removed his breather mask after entering the prison. He ignored the stares and whispers and approached the front desk. The guard didn't look up from his screen.

"I'm here to pay off someone's debts," Critch said.

The guard looked up then, recognized Critch, and after a brief startle, spoke. "Sure. What's the debtor's name?"

"Gabriel Lang. He's a Darion."

The guard swiped through several screens. "There he is. Looks like he owes eighty-three thousand two-hundred and fourteen credits."

Critch's jaw slackened. "Sounds like he had a good time in Devil Town."

"He did. He owes three casinos, two brothels, and a hotel." The guard then tapped a small pad on the counter. "You can send payment through here."

Critch tapped the amount on his wrist comm and held it near the pad, which chimed as soon as the transfer processed.

"Looks like we're all good here. I can have him brought to you."

"I'd rather go see him first."

"No problem." He returned to the screen in front of him before looking back up to Critch. "Vance is coming to bring you to your friend."

"He's not my friend," Critch corrected.

The guard hesitated but didn't speak.

A door to Critch's right opened, and a young guard stepped through. He couldn't have been over eighteen. He stopped when he saw Critch. "You're—"

"Here to pick up my crew member," Critch finished for him.

"Oh, yeah, of course. This way." He motioned to the hallway on the other side of the door. They departed the main entrance. Offices and interrogation rooms lined the long hallway, all with doors closed.

"My name's Vance," the guard said as they walked. "You saved me from being conscripted by the Collective."

"A lot of people fought for our independence. It wasn't just me, kid," Critch said.

"I know, but the vids always showed you and Aramis Reyne leading our armies on the ground. You on Terra, and Reyne on Darios. What was Terra like?"

"It was bad, kid. It was real bad."

They stopped at a security gate. Vance waved at the guard sitting behind a glass-like wall, who tapped on his screen. The gate opened, and they passed through into a wider hallway. This one was lined with larger rooms—a cafeteria, a rec room, and showers. Like before, the doors were all closed, likely a security protocol, leaving them alone in the hallway except for passing by another guard and through another security gate every so often.

Their boot steps on the polished stone floors were the only sounds before Vance spoke again.

"Did you know that you're still on the Collective's Most Wanted list?"

"Good thing I'm not planning to visit the Collective any time soon."

Again, silence as they turned left and arrived at a massive security gate. When the gate opened for them, they entered a large hallway with a ceiling easily two hundred feet high. The hallway was lined with stacks and stacks of cells. There was a stench of body odor in the air, which spoke to how dirty the inmates were, since all breathable air on Spate was constantly filtered and recirculated within each building.

Vance spoke. "When I was just a kid, I wanted to be a pirate. I was going to steal from the Collective to help out the colonists, just like you." He pouted. "But my dad wouldn't let me."

"Your dad sounds like a smart guy," Critch said.

The guard shrugged. "I became a cop instead. I figured it was the next best thing since I'd still be helping out my people. Okay, we're coming up on his cell column. It's this one up here." He stopped and pointed to a cell several floors above them. "Seven-Three-Three-Two. I'll bring it down and open the door for you."

Critch lifted a hand. "Don't open it just yet."

The cell Critch stood before was small, no more than four feet wide and eight feet deep, and identical to every other cell in Debtor's Row. The only things in the small white box were a slab with a thin mattress, a toilet hole, a drinking line coming out of the wall, and a frail occupant in gray coveralls. He was lying on the bed with his bare, calloused feet toward the hallway. The wall facing the hallway was clear, just like the security gates, with square holes throughout it, likely for air movement.

Vance tapped on his wrist comm, and the column of cells before them began to move slowly downward. The occupant struggled to raise his head, and Critch made eye contact with the inmate as the cell descended below the floor line. The yellow-eyed gaze he met was one of hope lost, and Critch was glad when the floor cut off their connection.

As each cell in the column descended, the inmates looked at Critch. Each had the same hopeless, lifeless gaze, regardless of their age. He'd seen that look before, back at the Citadel on Terra.

Critch bit back his anger. No one and nothing—no human,

no animal—should be caged like that, no matter what they'd done. His skin crawled, and he craved to leave. He found himself breathing harder, becoming claustrophobic, and then the cell column quit moving and Critch found himself eye-to-eye with Gabe.

Everything else forgotten, Critch stepped closer to the cell.

Gabe's dark hair, strong features, and endless confidence had drawn many women to his bed. This man had none of that. His head had been shaved, and malnutrition had turned once-attractive features into jutted cheekbones and a too-sharp jawline.

When Gabe recognized Critch, he shot up from the bed too fast. The man held on to the edge of the bed for support. Gabe's eyes were wild with fear as he looked from Critch to Vance.

"Relax, Gabe. We're just going to talk," Critch said.

After a long moment, Gabe seemed to accept Critch at his word and stepped up to the clear wall that stood between them. The pilot still had a hint of a saunter, but he didn't stand as tall as he had the last time Critch had seen him.

They stared at each other.

"I figured you'd find me. I thought it'd take you longer, but I knew you'd hunt me down," Gabe said.

"You stole my ship," Critch said.

Gabe shrugged. "I thought you were dead."

Critch shook his head. "Just because you left me for dead didn't make me dead."

"I never would've left if I thought you had a chance."

Critch narrowed his eyes. "Don't lie to me, Gabe. You've worked for me too long to be able to bullshit me."

Gabe winced.

"And you abandoned the rest of my crew at Rebus Station," Critch said.

Gabe held out his hands in placation. "There were plenty of

ships still at the docks for them to hitch rides out of there. I heard they stole a patrol ship and got away without a scratch."

"You're lucky none of them died on Terra. I wouldn't have been able to forgive that."

Gabe swallowed and looked away. He stared at his cell for a moment before turning back to Critch. "Get me out of here, and I'll take you to the *Honorless*. No one got hurt. Once you get your ship back, we'll call it even."

"Oh, yeah?" Critch asked.

"I had to run with her. The CUF was breathing down my neck. If I hadn't run, they would've blown her—and me—to shreds."

"Is that right?"

Gabe continued. "I saved her. It's because of me she's all in one piece." He hesitated. "At least, she was before I ended up in here."

"Let me get this straight. I let you out, and you take me to my ship," Critch echoed Gabe's proposal.

"Damn straight. Just get me out of this hellhole."

Critch studied his stray crew member. After watching Gabe squirm, no doubt wondering if Critch would make the deal or not, Critch motioned Vance, who opened the cell door.

Gabe looked at the guard before taking hesitant steps out of his cell. "Don't you have to pay off my debts to have me released?"

"I paid your debts when I arrived," Critch said. "I was counting on you wanting to make a deal."

"Oh, okay," Gabe said, his voice lacking its former confidence.

Vance led them back through the hallways and security gates. This time, he knew enough to not talk after hearing Critch and Gabe's conversation. Critch noticed the guard kept his hand near his gun, probably wondering if Critch would try to kill Gabe within the prison.

Critch wasn't an idiot. He wouldn't kill someone in a place filled with a colony's law enforcement. He was careful to not make any sudden or threatening moves.

When they reached the main entrance, Vance spoke to Gabe. "Stop by the front desk to have your tracker removed. You're free to go."

"Good riddance to this viggin' place," Gabe muttered.

Critch turned to Vance. "Take care of yourself, kid. And listen to your dad."

Vance smiled. "I will, sir. Thanks."

The officer at the front desk used a device that looked like a large pen to remove the tracker band on Gabe's ankle. He handed Gabe his wrist comm. Gabe frowned. "Where're my clothes, my gun?"

"All personal effects are given to charity. Weapons are reallocated to Spaten security forces. By law, we have to return wrist comms."

Gabe sneered while he snapped the wrist comm around his forearm. "Well, isn't that generous of you."

Critch unsnapped a breather mask from his belt and handed it to Gabe. "You're lucky you're even getting that. Now, let's go."

Critch pulled on his own breather mask, and they headed outside.

Gabe looked out at the desolate street. "You want me to call us a cab, or do you want to do it?"

"We'll walk," Critch said.

"It's a long ways."

"I don't care," Critch said.

"But I don't have any shoes."

Critch glanced down at Gabe's bare feet. "Good. Consider it penance for stealing my ship."

Gabe sulked but was wise enough to keep his mouth shut.

They walked down the steps of the prison and several paces alongside the street before Gabe rubbed his neck. He cleared his throat. A moment later, he coughed and stopped.

Critch stopped and watched the other man.

"I can't...breathe," Gabe said in between coughs.

"I know," Critch said.

Gabe's eyes widened as he looked at Critch. He lunged for Critch's mask, but the already weak man moved slower from lack of oxygen.

He spun to run back to the prison, only to be yanked back by Critch.

Gabe fell to a knee. "But...we...had a...deal."

"I held up my end. The deal was to get you out of Debtor's Row. I did. But that doesn't make up for you stealing my ship."

"You'll...never find...it."

"The impound lot? I already picked it up this morning."

Gabe realized he'd been set up all along and began crawling back to the prison. Critch watched him make it several feet before collapsing. Two guards came rushing from the prison.

Wheezing, Gabe yanked off his mask and sucked in air. His eyes bulged, and he scratched his throat. A second later, he was convulsing.

The guards reached them. One of them carried an extra mask and knelt by Gabe, whose convulsions had grown weaker.

"Bad breather mask," Critch said.

"If only he'd left his mask on, we could've swapped out masks and he would've been fine," the guard on the ground said, who Critch recognized from the front desk. "But as soon as he removed his mask, there was nothing we could do."

Gabe's body stilled, his eyes and mouth wide open. Already, his eyes were turning a deep yellow—what Spatens called fool's gold.

"Poor fool," the other guard said, and Critch recognized the voice as Vance's.

The pair made eye contact. Vance knew. Critch waited a moment to see if the guard would try to arrest him for murder, even though they'd never be able to prove a thing.

"Yeah," Critch said after a pause. "Poor fool."

CHAPTER 9

THE CASE OF THE MISSING BOTS

Tulan Port, Playa

REYNE WAS MORE than a bit surprised when Hadley returned an hour later with the items Boden had requested. At that time, Reyne's group was still talking with the construction crews in the stationhouse.

"I don't know what's going on, but I'm sure our Legacy Star bots were used in the attack," Hadley said as she handed a bot to Boden. "The manifests show five hundred spider bots arrived. I'm confident in that number because I manually looked over all supplies as they arrived. I ran pings on all the bots in operation, and the scans showed four hundred currently in operation, which means that we're missing one hundred bots."

"It seemed like a whole lot more than a hundred bots came after me," Reyne said as he remembered the attack. He shrugged. "But a hundred could be about right."

"Yes, but here's where it gets strange," she said. "Now, I oversaw my bots being sent to the docks this morning, and they seemed to be all there. I certainly would've noticed one hundred fewer bots out of two hundred and fifty. I called Simon to see if he noticed any of his bots missing, and he hadn't. And so I did a bit more digging, and I learned that only four hundred spider bots were initially deployed—two hundred to Simon and two hundred to me. I can only think that they were misappropriated sometime between being unloaded and being put into service."

"That's awfully convenient for you," Sixx said. "You didn't notice one hundred missing bots?"

She held out her hands. "My staff uncrated them. Yesterday was the first day of construction, things were hectic, and I guess I just didn't think of counting the bots as they were put into service. Believe me, Simon was just as surprised as I was to find that we're missing one hundred bots. We would've found the discrepancy soon enough. Production levels would be lower than they should be, but we haven't had a full day's stats to review yet."

Hadley then focused on Reyne. "I'm sorry for what happened to you. I want to see justice brought to whoever's behind this as much as you do, and I want things to work between us—between the Collective and the Alliance here at Tulan Port, I mean. Just let me know what I can do to help."

Reyne watched her for a moment. "I believe you, and I'm glad that you're helping us. But tell me, if the bots were stolen, how many people would have the software to be able to operate them?"

She replied. "Any Legacy Star employee, but they've all been thoroughly vetted for past felonies, and all of them volunteered for this project."

Boden stepped in. "These bots are pretty basic. Their operating software would be easy enough to download by just about anyone with some technical knowledge."

"Great. Then our list of suspects grows to anyone who had access to the crates," Reyne mused.

"Easy," Sixx said. "If what Hadley's telling us is true—and I'm not saying it is—we head down to the docks and review the camera feeds from when the bots arrived. Then we'll see who took the crate."

Hadley stiffened but didn't speak.

Reyne ignored Sixx and nodded to the bot in Boden's hands. "My guess is you won't find anything in there, since the others were taken a while back."

"Just the same, I think I'd better take a look," Boden said.

"You do that. But first, how about you go with Hadley and work through Legacy Star's personnel logs to look for any red flags." He paused and glanced at Hadley. "If that's okay with you?"

"Of course," Hadley said. "I'm happy to assist you in reviewing their work logs. However, I won't allow you to go through their confidential files. I respect their privacy."

"Thanks for your help. It means a lot," Reyne said, and nodded toward Boden. "You two better get started."

Boden took the hint and left with Hadley.

Sixx took a step closer. "Now that Hadley's gone, do you think she's involved?"

"I hope not," Reyne said. "Nonetheless, I'd like to keep our thoughts among ourselves for now."

"You have a plan?" Bree asked.

"The makings of one, starting with us heading down to the docks for the camera feeds."

"Let's go," Sixx said.

Reyne held up a hand. "It's not going to be quite that easy. The cameras are in place, but they aren't scheduled to be turned on for another three weeks, when the generators are installed."

Sixx and Bree frowned, and then Sixx spoke. "Ah, but the Legacy Star folks don't know that, do they?"

"They shouldn't, unless they've hacked my files."

Bree looked at her wrist comm. "Okay. You guys head to the docks."

"Where are you going?" Sixx asked.

She gave him an amused stare. "I need to pick up Lily from school."

Sixx's mouth formed an O. "Good idea."

"I'll swing by the docks and pick you guys up afterward," she said. "I know how much Sixx hates walking outside."

"It's true. I hate it," Sixx said.

"Be safe," she said.

He gave her a peck on the cheek. "What would be the fun in that?"

She left Reyne and Sixx to pull on their cold weather gear, and the pair made the walk to the docks. The walk was short but slow as they weaved around grinders and crews smoothing the hard surface found across Playa, the densest of all the colonized planets. Every time Reyne saw a bot, he tensed and patted the gun he'd holstered to his hip. He'd never go without carrying weapons again, no matter how safe Tulan Port may feel.

Reyne didn't speak to Sixx as they walked. The air was cold and made his teeth ache. Every now and then, he heard Sixx's muttered curses about the weather, and he wondered how long his friend would put up with Playa's temperatures before returning to his home world of Spate. Reyne knew Sixx's family still owned properties in Devil Town—Sixx would find an easy life there. Reyne supposed Sixx craved action too much to settle down, though he wondered if those cravings would mellow now that Sixx was living with Bree and his first wife's daughter, Lily.

A hard wind seemed to go all the way through Reyne's bones, and he made a mental note to check on the status of the tunnel's construction when he returned to the stationhouse. Reaching the docks was a relief, even though each docking bay was still exposed to the elements, as the silos had yet to be built.

They turned left, to where the Legacy Star contractors were building the Collective concourse. "You know, I have some mini-cams that are wireless. I could have them installed all along these walls." His words were muffled by his facemask.

"That may be a good idea," Reyne said, then nodded. "Let's go up there, just off where the crews are working."

The Legacy Star crews weren't far from the entrance. The humans were on the ramps, working with wires and electronics, while the bots scurried around the docking bay, digging out an oval opening in the ground.

They stopped below a nearby camera. Sixx pointed at it and spoke with a booming voice. "I'll pull the feed from this one, too."

Reyne tried not to grin at Sixx's overacting. At least the cameras were installed. He bellowed for effect, "Better pull them all." He motioned down the full distance of the concourse.

"I'm pretty good at this. Maybe I should get into acting," Sixx whispered.

"Stick with your current job," Reyne countered.

"Hey! What are you doing here?"

Reyne spun around to see Simon Tate rushing toward them. He wore a full-length, bright white coat that had no dirt smudges on it—nothing to hint that Simon had ever been near anything resembling work.

"I asked what you are doing here. This concourse belongs to the Collective. I run this area," Simon said.

"Correction," Reyne said. "This concourse is managed by the Collective. It belongs to Tulan Port, and as its stationmaster, *I* have ultimate authority here."

Simon's scowl was evident even through his goggles. "Well, what are you doing here?"

"I'm just touring the facilities and checking to see how construction is going."

"Construction is going fine. I'll even have this concourse done ahead of schedule. That is, if you don't keep bothering my crews and me."

"Bothering?" Reyne said. "Exactly how am I bothering anyone?"

"My crews are citizens. They aren't comfortable with colonists constantly looking over their shoulders."

Reyne held up a hand in defense. "Don't worry. I'll be sure to get out of your way as soon as my associate and I download the camera feeds."

Simon's eyes widened. "I heard those cameras weren't operational."

"Oh, they're operational all right."

Simon sputtered. "Oh, well, why do you need the feeds? Do you have nothing better to do than to watch citizens work?"

Reyne replied, "On the contrary, I heard that Legacy Star lost a hundred or so bots. I'm helping out by pulling feeds to see what we can see."

Simon glared. "Those missing bots are Legacy Star bots, which makes it Legacy Star business. I certainly don't need your help."

"No, but I'm glad to help, anyway. If we happen to have a thief in the area, I'm sure you would like to see them caught as much as I would."

"Fine. Have it your way." Simon grumbled something, then wagged a finger at Sixx. "And *you*. You just wait. I'm not done with you yet."

"You need to calm the hell down," Sixx said. "Seriously, whatever you think I stole, I don't have it."

Simon spun and strode away, his coat fluttering behind him.

"He's certainly not your biggest fan," Reyne said.

"He has anger issues," Sixx said.

"I don't trust him one bit," Reyne said. "You see how nervous he got when I said the cameras were working? Even if he didn't take those bots, he's done something he doesn't want anyone to see."

Sixx looked over Reyne's shoulder and grinned. "Hey, nut!"

"Dad!" Lily let go of Bree's hand and ran toward Sixx. Her thick coat made her look more like a brown snowball rolling toward them than a little girl. Even though he wasn't her father, she'd taken to calling Sixx "Dad" within a week of meeting him, and calling Bree "Mom" soon after. Reyne figured it was because she'd never had a decent father figure, and when one had stepped into her life with enthusiasm, she'd embraced the concept with just as much energy.

Sixx held out his arms and caught her up in them. "How was school?"

"It was great. I lost a tooth. See?"

As she went into the details of her tooth's demise, Reyne frowned at Bree, who stood frozen in place, focused on something in the area of the Legacy Star crews.

"Is everything okay, Bree?" he asked.

She snapped out of her trance. "Oh, nothing. I just thought I saw a familiar face." She brushed off the thought with a chuckle. "But that's impossible."

Reyne's wrist comm pinged. He read the message and his eyes widened. He turned to his friends. "Time to go. Boden says he's found the guy trying to kill me."

CHAPTER 10

UNWANTED HITCHHIKERS

Devil Town, Spate

CRITCH ARRIVED at the docks to find the *Honorless* sitting in a bay near the far end. Even after twenty years, his heart still leapt at the sight. She'd been a luxury yacht, belonging to some Alluvian fishing business magnate, when Critch commandeered her and gave her the name she now proudly bore. He'd spent ten years morphing her into the most feared pirate ship across the Collective, capable of taking on any CUF ship smaller than a destroyer, though he'd taken on one of those before and survived.

The *Honorless* dwarfed the passenger ships and transports docked nearby, making her impossible to hide while on the ground. She was meant to fly, and Critch was looking forward to getting her back up and into the black.

He wasted no time in filing his departure plan with Devil Town's dock control and boarding his ship. After scouring the ship and its systems, he was relieved to find that the greedy pilot hadn't screwed her up as badly as he'd expected. Critch's cabin remained locked, even though there were scratch marks around the keypad where Gabe had obviously tried to circumvent it in an attempt to break in. Several rifles were missing, likely pawned off for credits. And he'd already known both drop tanks would be missing, after hearing they'd been used up in one of Gabe's escapes from either the CUF or Critch's specters.

Critch took a seat in the captain's chair, and suddenly he felt like he was home. He closed his eyes and relished the sensations of being back in the only place that'd ever brought him peace. When he opened his eyes, he pulled out a tiny model of a ship and fastened it to a lever with a string. The ship was nothing special—it could be found in any toy shop on any planet. But this particular one bore great meaning. Having it on board was the closest thing to fulfilling a promise he'd made to a young Terran during the war. Kassel had dreamed of flying. The boy had reminded Critch of himself at that age. As fate turned out, Critch would never be able to teach Kassel how to fly, but he could at least see that a small part of Kassel would experience flight.

He abruptly refocused and began performing system checks. Both he and the *Honorless* needed to be off world. He felt claustrophobic on the ground. He had finished nearly all the pre-flight checks when he heard footsteps.

Critch spun in his chair and whipped out his handgun from his thigh holster.

The dock worker's eyes widened and his hands shot into the air. "Don't shoot me!"

Critch eyed the worker. The middle-aged man was terrified and had no sign of weapons on him. Critch holstered his gun before the man pissed himself. "What do you need?"

The worker lowered his hands slowly. "Ah-all your fuel tanks are full." He gulped. "Is there anything else?"

"I'm good. Just waiting for my final clearance codes."

The worker glanced over Critch's shoulder and nodded in the

same direction. "My boy has one just like that. You have a kid, too?"

Critch's eye twitched, and he glanced back at the toy ship. He shook his head. "It's from a kid I knew." He added, "We good here?"

"Oh, yeah. You're all set." The worker frowned. "Don't you have a crew? This is a big ship. You need—"

"I'm on my way to meet up with them." Critch's response was only a half-truth. While he was on his way back to Nova Colony to connect with what was left of his crew, the fact was that he'd been losing his crew one by one. First, Chutt. Then, Birk. Now, Gabe, though he wouldn't miss that piece of shit. He'd have to backfill the positions with fresh meat and spend years building trust and rapport. Sometimes he wondered if it wasn't time to hang it all up and settle down at Nova Colony.

He chuckled inwardly at himself. Like he could ever settle down.

The worker spoke again. "Well, if you need any crew members, I know of a couple guys looking for work."

"I'll keep that in mind. Now, I need to get going."

"Sure. Have a great trip. Come back to Devil Town." He spun on his heel and headed back down the hallway.

Critch turned back to his panel. A few seconds later, he heard footsteps once again. He sighed and turned around to face the dock worker. "Listen, I said—"

A cold object pressed against his neck. Critch froze. Knife or gun, he couldn't tell, not that either mattered, since both would guarantee death. He gave up the thought of reaching for his gun. The earlier feeling of being followed now made sense.

"Who are you?" Critch asked.

"My name doesn't matter. What matters to you is that I was sent by Mason." The voice was most certainly not that of the dock worker. This voice was smooth and steady.

Critch's jaw clenched. "Mason's dead."

"There's a new Mason."

Critch scowled. He'd expected his past to catch up to him, but he'd always figured he'd die on his feet with a gun in his hand. He took a breath and forced his body to relax. "Just get it done, already."

A bright flash, and then everything went black.

CHAPTER 11

ENEMIES, ENEMIES, EVERYWHERE

Tulan Port, Playa

REYNE SAT on the couch next to Bree. Sixx sat on the floor with Lily, who was busy playing a video game. The living room was small but had a homey feel to it, like the rest of the apartment Sixx shared with Bree and Lily. Sixx had never had a taste for decorating, so Reyne assumed it was Bree who'd found artwork and rugs to bring color to their stone living quarters. In fact, there were so many rugs and pieces of art, there was hardly any visible stone.

The front door opened, closed, and Boden came jogging into the room. "Sorry. I couldn't get a taxi," he said, panting.

"Hey, Uncle Tren," Lily said with a quick glance up from her game.

"Hey, Lily-bear," Boden said.

"You said you found something?" Reyne asked.

"Yes, I found him," Boden said, and then looked around. "I'm thirsty."

He disappeared into the kitchen and returned moments later

with a glass of water and a kitchen chair. He sat and then took a long drink.

"You were saying..." Reyne drawled out.

Boden swallowed. "I reviewed the summary report of personnel Hadley gave me. Everyone is clean, not a single red flag."

Reyne frowned. "I don't get where you're going with this."

"Well, there's no way any construction crew could be *that* clean, so I waited until after Hadley left for lunch, and then I stopped by her assistant's desk and asked nicely to see the files."

Boden was good looking and had charm, and he was excellent at applying that charm when he needed a Sweet Soy fix. That Boden had charmed someone to help out someone other than himself surprised Reyne. Maybe Boden truly was recovering from his addiction.

"I didn't get full access, but I didn't need it," Boden continued. "Once I saw his picture, I knew he was the one who tried to kill Reyne." He pulled out a piece of carbonized paper and handed it to Reyne. "Anyway, I could only get a hard copy, but you can see for yourself, it's him."

"Him who?" Bree asked.

Boden seemed startled by the question. "It's Laciam. Max Laciam. He's working at the docks under the name Mark Leonard."

Sixx cocked his head.

"You're saying the guy who was Corps General for a really short time is working a construction crew on Playa?"

"Yes," Boden replied.

"He was on Gabriela's Heid's crew before that," Reyne said without looking up from the paper. He stared at the picture of an athletic man with a strong chin and a bluish tint to his skin, marking him as a Myrad. His hair was longer, but his features still bore the stiffness and superiority of a CUF officer.

He passed the paper to Bree. "It sure looks like him."

"I agree with Sixx. It doesn't make any sense for him to be on Playa," she said.

"I'll ask Seda if he knows anything about what happened to Laciam after the war. Maybe he left the CUF."

"Knowing that hothead, he was discharged," Sixx said, and looked directly at Reyne. "But if he is here, it makes sense he'd come after you. After all, it was you who basically got him demoted from Corps General back at Darios."

"He did it to himself," Reyne grumbled, but he agreed with Sixx that Laciam had more than enough motivation to want to kill him.

Boden stood.

"Where are you going?" Reyne asked.

"I can't stay. I have a date with Melody," Boden said.

Bree cocked her head after handing the paper to Sixx. "Who's Melody?"

"Hadley's assistant," Boden replied.

"Boden, Boden, Boden." Sixx shook his head slowly, chuckling. "You're doing it all wrong. You're supposed to hightail it out of there once you get the information. Then you're supposed to avoid your mark, and that means never, *ever* go on a date with her."

"I had to do it. She asked before she let me see the files," Boden said.

"Then stand her up," Sixx said.

"Go out with her if you want to," Bree said. "I bet she has nothing to do with what happened to Reyne."

Boden put his hands in his pockets and shrugged.

"A word of caution," Sixx said. "Don't let her think you're taking her on a date just to get into her files."

"You're hopeless," Bree said to Sixx.

"What?" Sixx said. "I meant that things will turn nasty fast if she finds out she was being used. That's all."

"I know how to treat a woman," Boden scolded.

"Really? Because as long as I've known you, you've been pretty dang lousy at it," Sixx said.

Boden gave Sixx an amused look.

"Bye, Uncle Tren!" Lily yelled without looking up from her game.

"Bye, Lily-bear," Boden said before he exited through the door.

Sixx handed the paper back to Reyne. "If it's not Laciam, he's got a twin running around. I think we should pay him a visit tomorrow. And by 'we' I mean us and at least twenty of our armed security forces."

"Hold on a minute," Reyne said. "We have to think this through. If he sees us coming, he might take off running or, worse, do something stupid and try to hurt someone."

"Well, it's not like we can talk to Simon about interrogating Laciam. Simon's a weasel. If that guy in the picture is Laciam, then the two are connected somehow."

"Oh, shit." Bree's jaw slackened.

Lily pointed. "You swore, Mom!"

Reyne and Sixx watched Bree, whose back was now rigid.

Sixx rushed over to kneel by her side. "What's wrong?"

She looked down at the man with his hand resting on her thigh. "You're not talking about Simon *Tate*, are you?"

"Yeah." Sixx drew out the word slowly as his brow furrowed. "He's the Legacy Star leader in the docks. Why?"

"That's who I thought I saw at the docks," Bree said.

"I know Simon Tate." Lily scrunched her nose. "I don't like him. He was always telling me what to do. *Do this, Lily. Do that, Lily*," she mimicked the words of a man nagging her.

Bree let out a breath. "Simon Tate was Axos Wintsel's best friend."

Reyne looked at her. Bree had been an indentured servant under Axos Wintsel, her job was to keep Axos's guards "entertained." Axos was a Myrad with a mean streak—and Lily's father. Throttle had killed Axos after he'd kidnapped and tortured her, and Reyne wished he could kill him over and over again for hurting Throttle and Bree and for killing Sixx's wife, Qelle.

Bree shook her head as though trying to clear it before she spoke again. "I don't think he remembers me. After all, I was just one of the staff, so he probably wouldn't even recognize me. I bet he doesn't know that we know."

Sixx watched Lily play for a long minute before he lowered his forehead to Bree's knee. "He's here for Lily."

Bree frowned. "What are you talking about?"

Sixx looked up. "He told me I stole something from him. I didn't take it as a big deal because, let's face it, I've stolen from a lot of people. But now it all makes sense. It's the only thing that makes sense" He took Bree's hand. "We've got to get Lily as far away from here as possible, and we've got to do it fast."

CHAPTER 12

DANGEROUS COMMITMENTS

CUF Armada, outside Myr

ANDERS LOOKED across the room at the CUF's twenty-two commandants. Several wore concerned expressions, several others looked at him with confidence because already they knew why they'd been invited.

"Thank you for coming today," Anders began. "As you know, I've never held a face-to-face meeting with my entire senior staff before, but I believe the importance of today's discussion demands an in-person meeting. You may have heard that the *Unity* and the *Littorio* and their complements are undergoing renovations. That is true. However, those renovations are not to improve their fighting capabilities, but rather to repurpose those ships for deep space exploration. They will be the beginning of a new branch—the Collective Exploratory Forces."

Some brows furrowed, while others rose. He imagined many were surprised that they—the CUF's most senior-level officers— had heard nothing of a new branch.

Anders continued. "Parliament has rejected my course of action, but I reject Parliament, as it has not served the needs of its citizens for some time. Therefore, I've taken it upon myself to make the hard choices needed for the Collective's long-term survival. Without the colonies, Alluvia and Myr are struggling, and will continue to do so. I've learned that the Alliance of Free Colonies has already sent a colony ship outside our system, which means the Alliance will grow and accumulate resources while the Collective stagnates.

"While the CUF is crucial to the Collective citizens' protection, Parliament has no vision for the Collective's future. That's why I'm establishing a new military branch. Beginning today, one-third of the CUF's ships will be reallocated to the Collective Exploratory Forces. All personnel have the opportunity to remain within the CUF or transfer to the CEF to crew the colony ships. As the CEF is a long-term mission, families of personnel may of course join them on board the colony ships. I will command the CEF at the helm of the *Littorio*, and I expect Parliament will select a new Corps General to command the CUF. Before I continue with my plan, what questions do you have?"

The room erupted, just as Parliament had, only the officers soon found order and directed questions and concerns at Anders for the next three hours. After the questions evolved into conversation and opinion, Anders brought the room back to him by having assistants hand out thick packets detailing his plans and next steps for the CEF.

"I appreciate your insight and opinions. The Collective Exploratory Forces is here, regardless of what Parliament has to say about the matter. Tomorrow, each of you, as well as every active dromadier, has an individual choice to make: Remain serving the CUF and stay here within the Collective, or tour other star systems in search of new colonies as part of the CEF.

Every dromadier will receive an announcement and packet outlining their options tomorrow morning."

Anders rubbed his hands together. "Now, return to your ships and communicate what you believe necessary to your staff. While I'd prefer you to leave Parliament out of this, I have no doubts that they'll soon learn of my actions. They will likely order you to prevent the CEF from proceeding with its mission, but I warn you, should you attempt to use force on Collective ships and citizens, retaliation will be swift and extreme. My efforts are to ensure the Collective has a future, and I will not let shortsighted politicians get in my way. Is that understood?"

Agreements came from most of the officers, though a few remained silent. Those were the ones Anders had expected to face off against. He stood. "You have a lot to think about and a lot to communicate to your crews. You'd better get started."

As the room cleared out, Anders thought through who would join him in the CEF. Four of the officers were Founders, and another two were close friends, giving him enough leaders for the colony ships. Of the remaining sixteen, he expected a few would join his cause. His greater concern was the ones who'd side with Parliament and would consider using force against their own compatriots. The longer the colony ships remained within the Collective, the greater the danger they were in. That's why he intended to have the colony ships depart the Collective within a week.

CHAPTER 13

COLD VENGEANCE

Tulan Port, Playa

REYNE ROCKED in his desk chair as the call went through. His office still smelled of burnt metals, but it was at least functional once again. The air vent had a rilon grate over it, but he'd pushed a chair against it as well.

When the call picked up, Seda Faulk's face appeared on the screen.

"Reyne, you've got perfect timing. I was going to call you shortly."

"Do you know what happened to Max Laciam after the war?" Reyne asked bluntly.

Seda seemed taken aback, then regrouped. "Laciam? The Myrad who was Corps General?"

"That one," Reyne said.

Seda rubbed his chin. "I believe he was quietly discharged after punching Corps General Anders. Why do you ask?"

"Because he's here on Playa, and I think he's trying to kill me," Reyne answered.

Seda blew out a breath. "Well, I could see him blaming you for his fall."

"It wasn't my fault," Reyne said, exasperated that he'd told Sixx nearly the same thing. "Why does everyone think I'm to blame?"

"Because you didn't surrender when he asked you to, which caused him to make a very poor decision that nearly got you and everyone else at Sol Base killed. If he's come to Playa for you, be careful. Relations between the Alliance and Collective are still too bumpy. We can't afford a citizen as well-known as Maximus Laciam getting killed on Alliance soil right now."

"I know, but he may not give me any other choice."

"Find another choice."

"Trust me, I'll do what I can, but if I have to choose between his life and mine, you know what I'll do." Reyne sighed. "Why did you say you were going to call me?"

"Oh. There are some big things happening in the Collective. I'm calling a meeting, and I need all the stationmasters there."

"When?"

"In three days' time at Nova Colony."

Reyne frowned. "You need us to meet in person?"

"It's important enough that I believe it warrants a face-to-face discussion."

"Okay. I'll head out right after I have a word with Laciam."

Seda's gaze narrowed. "Exercise caution."

"I always do."

Reyne disconnected the call and Seda's retort. He leaned back in his seat, considering Seda's words. What did Seda have to talk about that warranted bringing all the stationmasters together? They already spoke weekly as it was, and there'd been nothing unusual on the last group call. With no ideas, he turned back to his screen. No new messages from Throttle. His heart ached. While he knew the transmission delays would grow wider, a part of him feared something tragic had happened.

He shook off the stress. He had enough to focus on, and three days to reach Nova Colony was tight. He didn't have time to dally. He tapped out a simple message to his crew: *We go to Laciam at 0930. Meet at my office.*

Affirmative responses came back swiftly. First Sixx, then Bree, followed by Boden.

He understood Seda's concern about relations, but Seda wasn't dealing with assassination attempts. Reyne thought long and hard about calling the local security forces, but they would be constrained by Alliance law in how they handled Laciam. And Reyne had no clear evidence that Laciam—assuming Mark Leonard was in fact Max Laciam—had tried to kill him.

If the night turned sour, Reyne trusted his crew, and only his crew, to handle the cleanup and cover their tracks. He armed himself to the teeth and waited for his crew. Sixx and Bree arrived first.

"Lily?" Reyne asked as they entered.

"She's safe. She's staying with a friend," Bree said.

"Good," Reyne said, and turned to see Boden stride into the office.

"How was your date?" Sixx asked with a crooked smile.

Boden grumbled something under his breath.

"Okay, everyone," Reyne began, "here's how this is going to happen. We're going to stop by Mark Leonard's residence to discuss a red flag on his file. Then we'll play it by ear. Hopefully, he's a good enough fellow to be honest. We arrest him if he's Laciam and get him off Playa as quickly as possible. I spoke with Seda, and he *really* doesn't want to have to deal with a dead ex-Corps General."

"Did you tell him that you really don't want to have to deal with someone trying to kill you?" Bree asked.

"I think I may have mentioned that once or twice," Reyne answered.

"I think we're on the same page," Sixx said. "Can we go do this already?"

The group drove to the Collective residences, located a mile from the stationhouse. Night had come and brutal cold along with it. They still had nearly four hours until the "dead hours," when no one would survive outdoors.

The residences had been built into the side of a dense hill in which the Collective had wasted no time laying its stake. The hill had natural caverns, making it easier and less costly to build out than many other sites. It also stood apart from the rest of Tulan Port, which Reyne suspected was the real reason the Collective had chosen the site.

With a guard post not yet established, they drove directly into the parking ramp and found a spot near a side entrance. Reyne scanned for cameras. He didn't see any, but that didn't mean there weren't any. The Collective had more advanced technology and could easily have discrete units already in place throughout its property. In this place, they'd have to play it safe and not do anything that could be misconstrued as Alliance aggression.

They entered the residences to find the hallway warm and well lit. The Collective had clearly seen to comfortable apartments before working on the docks and stationhouse. Reyne looked for a list of names and their residence numbers but found none.

"Names are listed on each touchpad," Boden said, several steps ahead of the rest of the group, and motioning to a touchpad on the wall next to a door.

Reyne frowned. "This could take a while."

And it did. They covered three hallways before reaching a door near the end of another hallway that read M. LEONARD above its touchpad.

Reyne stood for a moment before casting a glance to each of his team members. "Well, here goes nothing."

He tapped the keypad, and it lit up with a message that a bell was ringing inside the residence. They waited for a minute. Reyne noticed that both Sixx and Bree held their hands inside their coats. He had no doubt their hands were on guns already powered up to fire.

The touchpad chimed and instructions appeared on its gray surface. It read: *For identification, press your hand on this pad.*

Reyne lifted his hand, only to have it grabbed by Boden. "Let me," he said.

Reyne stepped clear from the door in case its occupant started shooting the moment it opened. He understood Boden's intent. Unlike the rest of them, Boden was a citizen and would be more likely to be seen in residences occupied by citizens, and it made sense not to have Reyne's identity logged into the system. Of course, all of that was assuming their entire team hadn't been picked up by cameras or microphones already.

Identity confirmed. Tren Boden. Alluvian, the touchpad read. It then chimed again, and the door opened.

Reyne tensed, expecting an attack. Instead, no one was there. Boden stepped into the doorway first and looked around. "I don't see anyone," he said and took a tentative step inside, then another.

Confused, Reyne followed. "Hello? Anyone home?"

Sixx and Bree entered, and the door closed with a *whoosh* behind them.

"I don't like this," Sixx said.

Reyne agreed. "Let's get out of here."

Bree pressed the pad next to the door. "It won't open."

"Let me." Boden rushed toward the door. He pulled out a screwdriver and went to work on the touchpad.

A skittering sound emerged from deep within the apartment, and then the noise grew, like a thousand crickets suddenly trying to chirp over one another.

Reyne's heart dropped, and he pulled out a gun for each hand. "Not again."

The dark hallway before them seemed to move and sparkle as robotic eyes lit every surface. Bots poured out in waves from the ceiling, walls, and floor. There were hundreds of the spider bots as well as the larger, round turtle-like bots used for drilling. It looked like the entire bot arsenal from both Legacy Star crews was coming at them.

Reyne, Sixx, and Bree fired at the onslaught while Boden worked at opening the door.

The bots were so tightly packed together that every shot was a hit, though each bot's central control system was such a small target within its hull that it almost always took more than one shot to take each one down. Reyne fired at a turtle bot and the shot ricocheted off its thick metal hull. These bots were designed to withstand tunnel collapses. Blaster fire did little more than leave scorch marks.

The long, spinning drills emerging from their fronts resembled jousting lances. Once the spider bots overwhelmed Reyne and his crew, it would take only a single hit from one of those drills to finish them off. On the bright side, they would likely be electrocuted by the smaller bots before that happened.

"Boden, get that door open," Reyne shouted.

"Working on it," Boden yelled.

"Viggin' bots!" Bree cursed above the gunfire as she fired at the faster bots.

Sixx kicked a bot across the room, but three more latched

onto his boot. They zapped at him with their small torches, and he jumped back. "Yeow!"

The room had become hazy and stank of burnt energy from the blaster shots. Even with the constant barrage of gunfire, the swarm was less than three feet away and closing the distance.

"Boden?" Reyne shouted.

"Almost there!"

There was a bright flash of light and a loud *zap*! Reyne turned to find the door open and Boden lying on the floor.

"Let's go! Reyne yelled.

They spun. Reyne and Sixx grabbed Boden's limp form, and the team sprinted into the hallway. Bree tapped the touchpad to close the door, but it remained open.

The bots poured out of the apartment and into the hallway.

"Run!" Reyne commanded.

They ran.

Along the hallway, a door opened. "What's going on out here?" a grumpy citizen asked while standing in his doorway. When he saw the bots, his eyes widened, and he disappeared back inside his residence.

Bots now flooded the hallway. Reyne and Sixx carried Boden while Bree fired at bots behind them. More doors opened. Most of them closed quickly when the occupants saw the battle taking place in the hallway.

They turned a corner and plowed into a woman. She fell.

"How dare you!" she scolded.

Bree went to help her up, but the woman yanked her hand away upon seeing Bree's weapons.

"Get up," Bree told her.

The woman didn't. By the time she saw the bots, it was too late. Already on the floor, they covered her within a second. She screamed as they shot electrical currents into her.

Unable to help, Reyne and his team turned away to see

Simon Tate running toward them. His terrified expression was focused on the woman. "No!"

Simon tapped his wrist comm, and suddenly all the bots halted, their lights dimming until they went dark.

Reyne and Sixx came to a halt, still supporting Boden, who moaned. Bree drew up alongside.

Reyne raised his blaster at Simon. "You had the off switch ready to go on your comm. That's awfully convenient." He tacked on for his team, "Looks like we've found our assassin."

"Worst assassin I've ever met," Sixx said.

Simon tore his gaze from the convulsing woman on the floor and turned his face—full of pure hatred—onto Reyne and his team, focusing on Sixx. "You...*you* did this."

Sixx chuckled. "Me?"

"Betts!" a man cried out and approached the fallen woman. Two more people entered the hallway and rushed to assist the woman. The first arrival went down to his knees and started knocking bots off the fallen. As he worked, he asked, "What happened?"

"You tell me," Reyne said. "We stopped by to pay Mark Leonard a visit and were attacked by your construction bots."

The newcomer frowned. "I've never heard of a Mark Leonard."

"Ah," Reyne said. "Let me guess. There's no Mark Leonard on this crew. His records were a ruse."

"These can't be our bots," another said. "Our bots stay at the job site."

"And I'll bet that you'll be short a whole lot of bots tomorrow," Bree said.

Hadley came running down the hallway, wearing a robe. She looked over the scene, then looked from Simon to Reyne. "What happened?"

"These colonists turned our bots against us," Simon said. "They released them in our residence hall."

"Good try, fella," Reyne said before turning back to Hadley. "I bet you can do a quick search to see who last programmed these bots."

"Give me a moment," Hadley said as her fingers flew over her wrist comm.

Meanwhile, Reyne holstered his blaster and tapped out a call to the local security forces. Boden groaned and then tried to stand on his own, but Sixx kept an arm around his friend.

"You okay there, buddy?" Reyne asked.

Boden nodded weakly. "That door gave me one hell of a jolt."

Hadley looked up and frowned at Simon. "Your credentials are the only ones logged on all the bots tonight. What were you trying to do, Simon?"

"Someone could've hacked the code to plug in my credentials," Simon retorted. Even he didn't sound convinced.

"I'll have techs run full diagnostics to verify the system wasn't hacked," she replied.

"Also have your techs run scans to see who created Mark Leonard's file," Reyne said.

"Who's Mark Leonard?" someone asked.

"He's no one," a woman said as she cautiously approached.

Hadley turned to the assistant. "Melody?"

Melody shrugged. "Mark Leonard was a test user I created for a system upgrade."

"System upgrade? I wasn't told about a system upgrade," Hadley said.

Melody nodded toward Simon, who had put several steps' worth of distance between him and the others. "Simon asked me to, and he thought it'd be funny to use ex-Corps General Laciam's picture."

Hadley snapped around to face her counterpart. "Simon, was

it you who sent Legacy Star bots against Stationmaster Reyne in his office, and again, tonight?"

Simon tensed. "No. I never sent them after Reyne."

"Simon," Hadley cautioned, "I will not help you if I learn that you lied to me."

Simon scowled and turned to Sixx. "You were supposed to be in the office."

Reyne froze. "All this time, you were after Sixx, not me?"

Simon gritted his teeth.

Sixx chuckled. "I hate to repeat myself, but you are, by far, the worst assassin I've ever seen."

Hadley put her hands on her hips. "Simon Tate, you must face consequences for releasing bots in our own residence halls."

Simon waved her off. "It wasn't supposed to happen like this! The stationmaster was supposed to send his chief of security to investigate Leonard. No one else was supposed to have been there."

"You're not making any sense," Hadley said. "Why in the worlds would Aramis send someone to investigate one of our crew, and one who doesn't even exist, at that?"

Reyne's sighed. "Because he wanted me to believe that Mark Leonard was Maximus Laciam, and that it was Laciam who was trying to kill me. Simon created the avatar to throw us off...and then used it again to draw us into a trap." He turned to Simon. "Your plan had potential, but it also had way too many holes and even more risks." He motioned to the woman on the floor, who'd begun to show hints of life.

Noise erupted down the hallway. Everyone tensed until Reyne saw that it was the Tulan Port security forces. Reyne pointed to Simon. "Arrest him, Simon Tate, for the attempted murder of me and my flight crew, along with, uh, Betts, there on the floor."

Simon chuckled. "You won't be able to hold me. And, as soon

as I'm out, I'll have the paperwork I need to take immediate custody of Lily Wintsel."

"The hell you say," Sixx said at the same time Bree said, "Never."

Simon sneered. "Oh, yes. While I'd be doing the Collective a favor by eliminating the worlds of that criminal," he pointed at Sixx, "even more important, I'll make sure that he doesn't have custody of a citizen's child." He lifted his chin. "Axos left me as Lily's legal guardian, and I will see to it that his last will and testament is fulfilled."

"You will *never* take Lily," Bree gritted out. "She has a home and a family who loves her."

Simon narrowed his gaze at Bree as his hands were banded behind his back. "You look familiar. Have we met?" A smile formed as recognition hit him. "Oh, yes. You worked for Axos. I had you one night."

"Watch how you talk to her," Sixx growled out, "or else I'll put a hole right between your eyes."

"Ah, you must care for her." Simon turned to Sixx, and his grin widened. "Tell me, how does it make you feel that she's serviced half of the Collective?"

"Sixx, don't let him goad you," Reyne cautioned. "He's going to jail. We'll see him face justice for what he's done."

Simon laughed. "You're foolish if you think the Collective doesn't have the real power around here." He turned to Sixx. "As for justice, whose side do you think they'll take? Lily's rightful guardian, who's a highly respected businessman, or a thief and a whore?"

Reyne noticed that the only thing keeping Sixx from lunging forward was that he still bore much of Boden's weight.

Sixx glared. "You just try to take Lily. You'll see the full extent of what I'm capable of then."

CHAPTER 14

LOOSE STRINGS

On board the Littorio, *near Myr*

CRITCH WOKE up with a headache worse than any hangover had ever given him. He opened his eyes, only to snap them closed due to the bright lights. The brightness hit him from every direction: above, below, and even the walls. There was only one place Critch knew to have 360-lights in all-white rooms—a prison cell on a CUF ship. He knew because he'd been in ones exactly like this on more than one occasion.

"Well, shit," he muttered, and rubbed his forehead with his hand. When the assassin had caught him, he'd assumed he was going to die...though he guessed he probably still was, since he was in a cell.

His wrist comm had been removed, as was done for any prisoner. He felt for his weapons and found nothing, as expected. His captors had even found the blade in the sole of his boot, leaving Critch both impressed with their diligence and disappointed at losing some of his best tools.

At least they'd left him with his clothes and boots.

A window in the door opened, and Critch looked, wincing in the light, to see Corps General Barrett Anders. "Ah, so you're Mason now? Couldn't come up with your own secret name?"

Anders ignored the comment. "Drake Fender, you've topped the CUF's most-wanted list for twenty years. That's quite the record, by the way. You had to figure that you'd get caught sometime."

Critch shrugged. "Evading the CUF hasn't exactly been challenging."

"Yet here you are, in my cell."

"That's because you cheated and hired an assassin."

Anders laughed. "A pirate accusing me of cheating. That's rich."

"Why'd you pick me up, Anders? Things getting a little dull around the Collective without colonists to push around?"

"On the contrary, things are rather exciting lately. You've been a loose string I've been meaning to pull for a long while. I'm running a bit short on time, and you're one criminal I don't plan to leave behind."

"Aw, let me guess. You've got some nasty disease that even Collective medicine can't help with. You've got a few months left to live, so now you're getting all nostalgic? Damn, if I'm not getting a little weepy."

The officer's lips curled upward. "Get weepy for yourself. This time next week, you'll be publicly executed for war crimes and piracy, though I care little about the piracy."

"War crimes? You mean, like when you bombed Tulan Base, where all the refugees were, and killed Vym Patel in the process?" Critch countered.

Anders sobered. "We all make hard choices in war, but some choices cross a line. You're being executed specifically for committing bioterrorism against the *Unity*, killing all 466 crew members on board as well as eighteen crew members on board the patrol ships sent in to investigate."

Critch chortled. "You're executing me for using the blight? How about Gabriel Heid and Michel Ausyar dropping the blight on Sol Base? They killed over seventy thousand colonists, and it wasn't even in a time of war."

"They're both dead and cannot be tried for their crimes."

"Ah, so I'm your scapegoat. You really think killing me will help you sleep at night?"

Anders shook his head. "No. But when I look at all those who pose a risk to the Collective, you're always at the top of the list. Your death will help a lot of citizens sleep better, and that makes the hassle of dealing with you worth it to me."

Critch leaned back. "I'm not saying I don't deserve to die, but I warn you that I'm a loose string that will cause a hell of an unravel in relations between the Alliance and the Collective. What do you think the colonists will do when they see the Collective coming after the torrent leaders who fought for their independence? Things are fragile. Killing me will shatter relations."

Anders raised his brows. "I think you greatly overestimate your importance to the Alliance."

"It's not me, personally. Hell, I never wanted the attention. But they've built me up into something bigger than life—Drake Fender and Aramis Reyne embody the torrent spirit." Critch paused. "Don't tell me, you're going after Reyne, too."

"Worry about yourself. After all, you're the one dying soon."

The window closed, leaving Critch alone in the bright cell.

Anders was a purist—Critch hated that type of person because they were impossible to bribe or sway. He had no doubt he was scheduled to be publicly executed, and there was no way to get out of it.

That left escape as his only option, but the list of challenges was awfully long. He had no idea where the *Honorless* was. He had no crew to come for him; hell, no one even knew where he was.

He frowned and thought for a moment. He had an idea. It was a long shot, like hitting-a-target-in-another-galaxy long shot, but it was also his only shot. He felt around on his right forearm, searching for the rice-sized tracker Seda Faulk had implanted to track him when he infiltrated the Citadel prison.

When he found the bump, he squeezed it until he felt it pop. If the thing still worked, it should now be shooting off a signal to Seda's wrist comm. If—and that was an even bigger *if*—Seda still had Critch's tracker programmed into his comm, then Critch's future would be in Seda's hands.

If Critch were a religious man, he'd pray. Instead, he began to brainstorm ways to get out of the damned cell.

CHAPTER 15

VACATION GETAWAY

Tulan Port, Playa

FOUR HOURS.

That was how long Simon Tate stayed in jail before Hadley showed up with papers from Legacy Star showing Simon's diplomatic immunity. Reyne couldn't say he was surprised. Wealthy citizens had always found ways to weasel around justice. He'd just hoped that it would've taken Simon Tate a bit longer to work the system.

Hadley shook her head. "I'm sorry. I absolutely believe Simon should face consequences for what he's done, but it's out of my hands. Legacy Star considers any public disgrace directed at one of their staff as a public disgrace to them. I suspect I have just choked my own career with them by not sequestering Simon away from security forces."

"They shouldn't punish you for Simon's actions."

She pursed her lips. "You've not spent much time in a corporation, have you?"

"Not a single day."

"You're fortunate." She glanced down at the papers and held them out toward him. "I suppose you should have these."

Reyne eyed them. "As soon as you hand those to me, I'm required by law to give those to the authorities."

She shrugged. "I assume that is the case."

He cocked his head. "Would you help if you could?"

"Of course."

"Then hold on to those papers for thirty minutes, at which time you can bring them back to my office."

"How will that help?"

"Just trust me."

She eyed him for a moment before she tucked the papers into her jacket. "Okay." She turned to leave his office, then paused, looking at him again. "I wasn't involved in Simon's schemes, though I should've known something was up. Even though he had nothing to do with the war, it changed him. He became short-tempered and distant. Looking back, I suppose it all happened when his good friend died. I wish I would've figured it out before your friend and Betts were hurt. We're so lucky no one died as a result of his actions. I'm glad you're okay."

"Thanks."

She turned to leave.

"Hadley?"

She stopped and looked back at him.

"Would you like to go out sometime?"

She pursed her lips, fighting a smile that won, anyway. "I'd like that." She turned to go.

He grinned and watched her leave. After she was gone, his smile faded, and he tapped his wrist comm. "I'm on my way. Are we all set?"

"We're ready," returned Sixx's voice.

Reyne hustled from the stationhouse and directly to the private docks where the *Gryphon* waited. He jogged up the ramp, even though his arthritic joints were aching from the bot attack the night before. As soon as he was on board, he closed the door and headed straight for the bridge.

Sixx jumped up from the captain's seat as soon as Reyne entered the bridge. "Flightplan's booked, and we've got clearance from dock control."

"Good," Reyne said as he took the pilot's seat. He'd piloted the *Gryphon* the first fifteen years, but then he'd turned the controls over to Throttle to build her skills. She'd quickly acclimated to the controls and within five years had exceeded Reyne's skill. She'd always been a natural when it came to piloting a ship. He wondered if she was still alive.

"You okay, boss?"

"Yeah. Just appreciating being back with the old girl again." He switched focus to the instruments. He powered up the nav engines and ran system checks. He tapped Boden's comm. "Everything's showing green up here. How's it look back there?"

"Everything's green, but the right nav engine is within a few hundred hours of needing an overhaul."

"She has a few trips left in her then." Reyne glanced over at Sixx. "Lily?"

"Bree's with her in her bunk."

"Good." He then transmitted to the ship. "Buckle in everyone. We're taking off momentarily for a nice little vacation getaway to Nova Colony."

After one final glance over the system checks, Reyne transmitted to Tulan Port's dockmaster. "Dock Control, this is Phantom cruiser Playa-Seven-Five-Five-One-Bravo. Ready for departure."

"Phantom cruiser Five-One-Bravo. You are cleared for immediate launch from launchpad Charlie Zero Four. Control has been transferred to you. Have a nice flight."

"Thank you, Dock Control. Have a good day." He applied

power to the engines and tapped the launchpad release. With a roaring rumble, the *Gryphon* shot upward from the tube and into Playa's atmosphere. The ship rocked as it climbed through the air and smoothed out as soon as it broke through and entered the black.

He glanced at the instruments and noticed the time. Hadley would be returning to his office, and instead of finding Reyne, she'd meet his assistant, who would tell her that he was now on a business trip for at least a week. He hoped Hadley would understand.

Reyne knew that the moment they returned, Simon Tate would be marching straight into his office with a court order granting him custody of Lily. He could only hope he'd have something figured out by then.

The three-day flight to Nova Colony was uneventful, which felt strange after being hunted for so long. Nova Colony, a large asteroid within the Space Coast asteroid belt, always required the pilot's focus to navigate, and Reyne found himself enjoying a little back-to-basics flying.

By the time they docked and passed through the airlock, Seda Faulk was waiting for them.

"You're the last to arrive," Seda said. "I heard you've been giving Legacy Star a bit of trouble."

Reyne grunted. "If surviving assassination attempts is giving them trouble, then sure."

They smiled then, and clasped each other's forearms in the standard colonist greeting.

"That sounds exactly like the Legacy Star I'm familiar with," Seda said. Upon seeing the young girl, he bent down. "We haven't met before. Are you on Reyne's crew?"

"Yup!" She smiled. "I'm Lily Sixx, and I'm Uncle Aramis's computer expert."

"Really? That's a tough job, I bet."

She blew out a breath. "It is. I don't get paid enough."

Seda smirked and returned to full height. He held out a key to Sixx. "It's an apartment on level G. It's under the name of one of my corporations, so no one should track you to it."

"Thanks," Sixx said. "Hopefully we won't need it very long."

"It's yours as long as you need it."

Seda embraced Bree. "Good to see you again."

"Likewise," she said.

Seda turned back to Reyne. "Is that your entire crew?"

"Boden's taking care of post-flight checks. And you already know about Throttle..."

"How's the trip going?"

"Good," Reyne answered too quickly.

Seda eyed him. "I see. Well, make yourself comfortable. The meeting starts in two hours."

CHAPTER 16

DEATH BY COMMITTEE

Nova Colony, within the Space Coast asteroid belt

REYNE SAT at the large table in Critch's office on Nova Colony. Critch was still out searching for the *Honorless*, leaving Nova Colony and his home in Seda's hands. Reyne suspected Critch wouldn't be gone for long—Reyne had heard that Seda had quickly grown accustomed to Critch's accommodations, which would no doubt irritate Critch. Seven people sat around the table, including the other stationmasters: Joe Thomas of Rebus Station, Hatha Satine of Sol Base, and Margerite Dubois of Devil Town. Hari, of course, sat next to Seda as his ever-present second-in-command. Shauna Fields filled the last chair. Reyne had met her during the war when she was a conscript on a CUF ship. She'd quickly developed a reputation as a capable leader, and he'd heard her speak on several calls with the other station-masters.

"Thank you for joining me in person. I know how much it takes for you to make the journey," Seda began. "It's been several months since we've had an onsite meeting, as we've all been incredibly busy getting the Alliance of Free Colonies off the ground. We have an offer from a group of private investors in the Collective that can help us with the one thing we all desperately need more of, and that's money."

Hatha held up a finger. "I'll stop you there, Seda. While I agree we're all currently bootstrapped, I thought we all agreed that we'd be developing Alliance currency so that we're no longer dependent on Collective currency."

"And I'm not inferring that we break from that strategy. The proposal I've received will help build up our economic strength. The Alliance currency, once we develop it, will be more comparable in value to that of the Collective's."

"What's the proposal, Seda?" Joe asked.

"It's a one-time mass purchase, off the books for all Collective trade, and to be transacted this month. Ten billion credits to each fringe station for the purchase of fuel from Terra, cavote from Darios, blue tea from Spate, and rilon from Playa. Hari is sending you the contractual details to your wrist comms now."

All four stationmasters reviewed the proposal on their small screens. Reyne's jaw slackened. He cocked his head at Seda. "Those numbers are higher than any of us have seen before, except for maybe you, and you think the Collective won't notice?"

"Oh, they'll notice all right, but as it's a private deal, they have no say. It's a huge opportunity for each of your colonies."

"It's also a huge demand," Margerite said. "It'll wipe out our warehouses. Anyone else with contracts would have to be delayed. We'll lose money if we have to pay for breaking contracts."

"Any money you lose will be drops from the bucket of what you'll make," Seda said.

"The Collective tariffs will put a dent in our earnings," Hatha said.

Seda shook his head. "They have attorneys in place to handle the tariffs. Consider them excluded from your transactions."

Reyne leaned back. "You know, whenever I hear something too good to be true, it usually is. That some mysterious group of private investors jumps in to help us when we need it most seems awfully suspicious." Reyne frowned when his words brought forth memories and trepidation. "Speaking of mysterious groups, this isn't connected to the one you were involved in a while back, is it?"

"What group is that?" Joe asked.

"No, it's not," Seda said. "I broke my affiliation with that group before the war."

Reyne wasn't so sure he believed Seda. "Well, I still think it's mighty suspicious for a group to pop up out of nowhere. Why would a group have an immediate need for so many resources?"

Seda inhaled deeply. "As we speak, a significant faction is breaking off from the Collective. Under the command of Corps General Barrett Anders, they are repurposing no small part of the CUF armada into colony ships. Parliament does not support this action, which is why they must depart with haste. Now I hope you can see why time is of the essence."

"The Collective is entering a second civil war," Hatha said.

"Let's hope it doesn't come to that," Seda said. "There are many citizens who feel that the Collective must expand in order to thrive. They have no intention of raising arms against their compatriots. They are simply volunteering to expand the Collective."

"Without Parliament's approval," Reyne said. "That makes them traitors who are stealing CUF property. We saw how well that worked out when Commandant Heid ran off with the *Arcadia*."

Seda sighed. "This is different, in that as soon as they have the necessary supplies, the colonization fleet will be heading away from the Collective and out of our system."

"What's to stop the Collective from coming after anyone who helps these people? By all rights, we're allying ourselves with their enemy the moment we accept the money."

"Because the Collective needs the colonies far more than we need Alluvia and Myr. If the CUF attempts to instigate a fight with the Alliance, they'll have both their own ships as well as our new military fleet to face."

Reyne jerked. "What are you talking about?"

Seda motioned to the woman at his left. "Captain Fields has accepted the position of Commander of Alliance Marines. Commander, if you please."

She stood. "The Collective has the CUF. The Alliance has nothing. We need a military force capable of standing against the Collective, should they choose to try to reclaim the colonies. Within a year, we expect to have two warships, six destroyers, and three dozen gunships. One destroyer is nearly complete."

Reyne frowned. "Where are you building these ships? Why haven't we heard of this until now?"

"We're building the ships at an asteroid within the Space Coast. Seda and I believed it was imperative to keep the early development of our infrastructure quiet to ensure the Collective did not learn of our intentions and act before thinking. Now that we have a good start, we'll soon open up recruitment with a training facility on Terra."

"Where on Terra?" Joe asked.

"At my old landing strip," Seda said. "It's not within Rebus Station's jurisdiction, therefore, I didn't need to inform you."

"But it's called common courtesy," Joe retorted.

"I don't like being out of the loop," Hatha said. "And all of a sudden, I feel like a puppet getting my strings pulled. It feels a lot like when Sol Base was a part of the Collective."

Seda leaned forward. "I knew this would be a challenging conversation, but you forget our roles—all are important, but they are different. I'm president, and accountable for the Alliance of Free Colonies. Everything I do is to strengthen the Alliance. You're stationmasters, responsible for the livelihoods of each of your colonies. If anything at any point impacts your colony, you'll be the first to know. Once established, the Alliance Marines will protect all the colonies from outside aggression. To put it bluntly, Commander Fields's job, and the forming of our military force, is outside your purview. However, feel free to contact the commander or me whenever you have questions. I know you have enough on your hands already, such as making a ten-billion-credit decision."

Margerite spoke. "As you all know, I was a madam before I became a stationmaster. Accepting money from those I'd rather not was necessary for staying in business, even when that money brought problems. I see it no different for Devil Town's prosperity. I'll accept the offer on behalf of Devil Town. They'll have enough blue tea to last a thousand people ten years without water."

"Sol Base still has plenty of food stored in the warehouses from when the blight hit," Hatha said. "This will give us a chance to clean out all that food without having much impact on our current contracts."

"We'll barely be able to meet their demand, if it's even possible," Joe said. "Seda, you own the juice plants. You know the production levels. What they're asking for may be more than we can pull together."

"I am quite aware of production levels, and my new plants won't be opened yet. That's on me," Seda said. "As soon as I received the proposal, I opened extra shifts to ensure we're running at maximum capacity every hour of the standard thirty-hour day. We'll at least give them what we can. I suspect Reyne is in a similar situation."

Reyne nodded. "We sent much of our extra inventory with the *Gabriela*, and everything else has been going towards the building of Tulan Port. I'm not sure how much we can scrounge together."

"What if you give them semi-processed rilon?"

"Carbon fiber? I'd have to check with the production plants, but I know creating the carbon fiber is the fastest part of the process. If they're willing to take weaker production materials for the same price, we can provide them with all the carbon fiber they can carry." Reyne held up a hand. "It looks like we're all in for this get-rich-quick scheme, but we'd better sleep with one eye open for the next year, because we're not making friends with the Collective by doing this."

"I know accepting the proposal presents us with risk, but the money can be used to establish a strong economy across the Alliance far faster than the scraping by that we've been doing. I'll notify Barrett Anders immediately after we break. Expect to see the news covering the colony fleet's movement." Seda took a deep breath before continuing. "Now, I have some bad news to share. A friend of mine on the *Littorio* has notified me that Drake Fender, who many of you know as Critch the pirate, has been arrested and is scheduled for execution."

Gasps erupted.

"When?" Reyne asked.

"I believe Anders has scheduled his execution for two days from now."

"We can't allow it to go through. Fender is a war hero," Joe said.

"He may be a war hero to the Alliance, but he's committed war crimes against the Collective.

"You could say the same of all of us," Reyne countered. "You see how Critch is now? That's how I used to be. A man can change, and I sure plan to give Critch that chance."

"You may have been through a dark time once, but we must all admit that Critch has spent more of his career as a pirate than as a war hero," Seda said.

Reyne scowled. "You say that while you're sitting around Critch's table in Critch's office and drinking his whiskey."

Seda pursed his lips. "If we try to intervene, then we could risk our proposals. Are you saying you're willing to risk ten billion credits for the life of one man?"

Reyne stood. "Absolutely, unequivocally, emphatically *yes*. He's saved all our lives here, mine on more than one occasion. There's no way we can leave him to die."

"I agree," Joe said. "I will be hung in the streets of Rebus Station if the colonists there learn that I could've saved Drake Fender and instead sold my soul to the devil."

"Colonists will never know that we were even aware of Critch's imprisonment prior to his execution," Seda said.

"Bullshit," Reyne said. "Colonists are smart; they'll figure it out, and then we'll be in deep shit. I'm not saying Critch hasn't crossed lines here and there, but haven't we all in the name of independence? I just know that Joe's right. If we allow Critch to be publicly executed, then we'll be next. The solution's easy. Anders brought us the trade proposal, and Anders is the one planning to execute Critch. I say we accept the proposal under the constraint that Marshal Drake Fender is returned to us, unharmed."

"Unfortunately, Barrett has already made it clear that he is unwilling to stay Critch's execution. I contacted him as soon as I learned of Critch's situation, and Barrett was quite adamant. It seems he believes Critch is a continued threat to the Collective's well-being."

"I bet Anders gets more flexible when he has no supplies from the Alliance for his colony ships," Reyne said. "Listen, I don't agree with Critch all the time. Hell, we rarely agree on anything. But the fact remains that Critch—Drake Fender—has dedicated his life to the colonies. To the colonists, he's the personification of the torrent ideal. If we side with the man who's kidnapped and going to kill him, we will lose the complete support of the colonists. Those billions of credits filling our pockets won't do anything to help the economy when we're at civil war with ourselves."

Hatha sighed. "You overestimate his worth. I believe it's in the best interest of the Alliance to allow the execution to proceed without intervention."

"I like Critch, I really do," Margerite said. "But I'm with Hatha. He's just one man, while the credits can benefit thousands of people."

"Anders doesn't get anything from Playa," Reyne said. "Not without Critch."

Seda narrowed his gaze at Reyne. "The proposal is for all four colonies. We're not omitting one because you disagree with something taking place outside the proposal."

Reyne shot him a hard look. "Oh yeah? Then how are you getting Playa's resources?"

"I am president," Seda said. "The needs of the Alliance must outweigh the willful segregation of a single colony."

"President? You're starting to sound more like a dictator to me."

"You know everything I've done is to benefit the colonies," Seda said. "We've fought together. We want the same thing. But our hands are tied. I only told you all about Critch because I wanted you to hear it from me before you saw it on the news."

Reyne watched him for a moment and headed toward the door.

"Reyne," Seda called out. "Give me your word that you won't try to do something stupid."

"You have my word," he said and walked out of the meeting room. He wasn't going to do something stupid. He was going to do something heroic and incredibly crazy.

He tapped his wrist comm to call his crew to him, and he found them waiting for him at the Uneven Bar.

"Anders is going to execute Critch," Reyne said bluntly. "Now, you don't have to go with me—"

"I'm in," Sixx, Boden, and Bree said at the same time.

Reyne held up a hand and looked from Sixx to Bree. "What about Lily? She can't come on this mission."

"Layla will watch her," Bree said.

"I hate to say this, but what if something happens to both of you out there?"

Sixx and Bree looked at each other as though having a conversation no one else could hear.

"We'll figure it out," Bree said quietly.

Reyne gave an understanding nod. "Okay."

"Reyne, wait."

He turned to see Hari approach.

Reyne scowled. "What? Did Seda send you to make sure I behave?"

"Quite the opposite in fact," she said. "Whatever you're planning, I'm in."

He watched her dubiously. Hari had always sided with Seda. That she'd sacrifice years of friendship made him suspicious, but then again, the Hari he knew had always been a straight shooter, so maybe she'd come on her own volition.

"All right. You're in," Reyne said.

"All the specters will be on board, I'd bet," Sixx said.

Reyne nodded. "Once we figure out where Critch is—"

"He's on the *Littorio*," Hari said. "His tracker is still online, and I have it programmed into my wrist comm."

"Okay." Reyne took in a deep breath. "Here's what we're going to do..."

CHAPTER 17

A BID FAREWELL

CUF Armada, outside Myr

"WE CAN'T LEAVE YET. My wife hasn't arrived."

Corps General Barrett Anders turned to face the owner of AlluMyr, the Collective's largest interplanetary transport company.

"I'm sorry, Mr. Traveres, but you've had a year to coordinate. Unless she arrives within the hour, it's up to her to book a flight to meet up with us in the Alliance sector. You clearly have a transport ship capable of delivering her to our rendezvous coordinates." Anders turned away, only to have his arm grabbed.

"Wait a minute, General," Traveres said. "I've sunk every credit to my name into this trip. The least you can do is wait for Lenda."

Anders grew tired of catering to his wealthiest passengers. Each one seemed to think they deserved special treatment for contributions to the mission. "We are all thankful for your support, Mr. Traveres. However, you are not the only citizen to support our cause, and it's not fair to jeopardize the entire mission—and the lives of everyone on board these ships—by waiting one more hour for your wife. As I said before, if she doesn't make it before we leave the Collective, then it's up to her to make it to the Alliance. Though, if she's not on board now, I wonder how much she really wants to go on this trip."

"Lenda wants to go," he snapped. "But she doesn't want to leave her parents behind. She's been trying to talk them into coming. She said she'll be here within two hours."

Anders clenched his jaw. "We've talked about this. This trip will take years if not decades. The last thing anyone wants on this ship is a passenger who doesn't want to be here. And she has one hour, not two."

He walked away from the businessman and hustled to the bridge. More people tried to stop and talk to him on the way, but he ignored them. They would have plenty of time to talk after they left the Collective.

When he reached the bridge, he locked the door behind him to keep out the civilians. He looked over his bridge crew before settling his gaze on his second-in-command. "Tully, how are we looking?"

The comm tech spun his chair to face Anders. "Commandants Smith and Lyness have reported in from their warships. Each of their complements is ready to jump at your command. However, the CUF armada is blocking our flight path. We still need to bypass them before we jump."

Anders nodded. "We won't know how they'll respond until we move, but you'd better advise our fleet that they have full authority to fire at any CUF ship that fires first."

He took a seat and scanned his comm panel to see the status of the eighteen ships—nearly a third of what had been the CUF armada—that composed the Collective Exploratory Forces: three warships, four frigates, and eleven destroyers, along with several dozen gunships and transports held within the larger ships' bays.

Twenty civilian transports were also accompanying the fleet. The number was higher than Anders had ever dreamed. When he'd first proposed colonization to the Founders, he'd never expected nearly the entire organization to volunteer to jump on board.

Through the Founders, he'd gained access to the Collective's wealthiest citizens and their resources. While he had some concerns that they were taking too much from the Collective, he knew that what he was doing was best for its long-term viability.

Confident that the colony fleet was ready, Anders tapped his comm channel and placed a call.

Seda Faulk's face appeared on screen. "Corps General, may I assume things are on track?"

Anders nodded. "Yes. We move in thirty-six minutes and should arrive at the planned coordinates within six days. Will the colonies be ready to begin transferring the supplies by then?"

"Yes, and we'll have Alliance Marines in place to help protect your ships while you're in our sectors. However, two stationmasters have strongly voiced their opinions about you holding Marshal Drake Fender in your cells—they would like to withhold supplies until you release him."

"As we've already discussed, that is not happening. The war is over, but Drake Fender is not the type who'd care. No citizen is safe from him as long as he's alive."

"And, as I've already told you, Fender is a friend, and I don't stand with you on this. Should you execute him before the supplies are transferred, expect delays. Some delays could be significant. I caution you, if you execute him, you will complicate things."

Anders thought for a length. He knew the political quagmire he'd stepped into by arresting Fender, but he firmly believed that he could save hundreds, if not thousands, more lives by taking the pirate out of the picture. "Make no mistake, I will execute Drake Fender for his war crimes, but I can hold him until after our business is conducted and the colony ships depart all Alliance sectors. That way, justice is done while not prickling patriotic emotions. Do you believe that will suffice?"

"It's acceptable," Seda said. "I'll see you in six days."

"See you then."

The call disconnected.

Anders had no doubt that Seda was trying to control him. Seda was a politician and knew that compromises were a part of every step of progress, yet he was running the Alliance like a business, trying to bypass any compromises to get every deal in his favor. Seda had taken advantage of Anders's time constraints and seen to it that the colonies were overly compensated for their supplies. That Seda was also trying to steer Anders in how justice would be carried out frustrated him. If Anders remained in the CUF as Corps General, he'd seriously consider going after *every* torrent leader, including Seda Faulk and Aramis Reyne. The only reason he hadn't sent Ranger after them already was because they seemed to be following the laws. He was starting to reconsider that decision.

He sent an encrypted message to Ranger to meet at the rendezvous coordinates. It never hurt having an ace up one's sleeve.

"Sir, we're at the ten-minute countdown," Tully announced. "Do you have any announcements to the fleet?"

Anders looked up. "No. Everyone knows their job. Make the countdown audible throughout the ship." He then looked out the front screen, which spanned the entire wall. Space beyond them was displayed as though the screen were a window. They still sat facing the CUF armada outside Myr's EMP nets in a face-off. They'd been in this configuration since an hour after Anders made the announcement to his officers. Few dromadiers from the other ships had joined Anders's fleet, and he suspected the captains had been ordered to keep anyone from leaving.

Anders, on the other hand, had encouraged his crew members to leave his fleet and return to the CUF, because if they chose to stay, there would be no turning back. The CUF had allowed civilian transports through their blockade, likely because Parliament was afraid of firing upon its most powerful citizens.

At the one-minute mark, Anders transmitted to the full armada. "This is Corps General Barrett Anders speaking to the armada of the Collective Unified Forces. The colony ships are about to embark on a journey to expand the Collective into new systems. When we return, we will return the ships, along with news of new Collective colonies. There is no one on board who is here against their will. Please do not stand in our way. Let us look to the future together."

The countdown chimed. "It's time," Tully said.

"Let the *Littorio* lead the way," Anders said.

The armada before them didn't move, even though the distance between them diminished. He constantly scanned the ships before them, looking for any flash of light to signal that a ship had fired upon the *Littorio* and her complement.

"So far, so good," Anders said under his breath as they closed the gap. While the armada had formed a blockade, the ships weren't connected to each other. Instead, they stood with nearly fifty kilometers of open space between them, the minimum acceptable distance as per CUF standards. Anything less than that posed a risk when a ship fired a projectile weapon, as the backlash would move the ship some distance before its engines readjusted its position. It wasn't like ships in space could drop anchors.

Given how long it took to make even the smallest adjustments in direction, Anders would've been far more comfortable having a couple hundred kilometers open. As it was, every colony ship had to be highly precise in order to move through the armada without ramming into another ship.

Tension tightened Anders's muscles as they approached the armada. He'd chosen to lead the fleet because, if the armada was going to fire upon them, it made sense they'd fire upon the lead.

By the time the *Littorio* reached the armada, Anders's fingers were cold from squeezing the edges of his armrests. To his left on the view screen stood the *Unity*, the apex of the armada. To his right stood the *Qin Shi Huang*, equally as impressive. If the warships fired upon the *Littorio* as it passed between them, Anders would never be able to evade in time.

This was the greatest risk in the entire mission, when Anders would learn if the Collective would allow a portion of its citizens to embark on an exploratory mission. He knew several of his passengers had padded the pockets of senators to help ensure that there wouldn't be a majority vote to fire upon the fleet. But the CUF didn't need majority rule; all it needed was a perceived risk to the Collective in order to attack.

Anders let out a breath as they left the two warships behind them.

"I can't believe we made it through," Tully said.

"Prepare for jump the instant the rest of our fleet is through the blockade," Anders said. "Put the reverse view on screen."

Now he could see the fleet behind them, all flying through the spaces between the CUF ships. Anders became more and more confident as the other two warships and all the frigates made it through, unharmed.

The smaller destroyers and transports looked like a swarm of bees buzzing through the armada's openings. Flashes of light danced along the sides of the CUF ships. Seconds later, ships exploded, the fires dissipating in the vacuum of space nearly as quickly as they'd erupted.

"They're shooting at the transports," Tully exclaimed.

Anders grimaced. A rock settled in his gut. "They're worth

nothing to the CUF. Plus, that way, they can say they tried to stop us. Damned politicians."

The remaining destroyers and transports zigzagged through the armada and jumped the moment they were clear.

"How many did we lose, Tully?" he asked.

"It looks like all but eight transports made the jump. Five of those were destroyed. Three are damaged."

His jaw tightened. "We expected ten percent losses. It doesn't change our plans. Make the jump."

"Sir, what about the three ships still out there?"

He saw a couple ships were crippled, and he hoped the CUF would give the poor souls on board a chance. He shook his head. "If we stay, we won't make it out of here. They have the coordinates. Any survivors can hop transports to rendezvous with us in the Alliance. Now, let's get out of here and to the Alliance. We've got a big trip ahead of us."

CHAPTER 18

SHIP RAT

On board the Littorio, *en route to the Alliance*

CRITCH COULD TELL the ship had gone to jump speed when the walls vibrated and he was sent tumbling off his bunk.

"A little notice would be nice next time," he grumbled as he rubbed a bump forming on the back of his head. It didn't make any sense for a CUF ship to go to jump speed unless it was after someone...or running from someone. But since Anders was the Corps General, he assumed it had to be the former.

As he lay on the floor, he realized that his security guard would've left his cell to buckle in for the jump. The thing about jump speed was that the crew generally had all sorts of safety checks to go through before and after each jump. This would be the time they'd be least focused on a prisoner.

He sat up and considered his options. He'd escaped from CUF cells before, and there was really only one way to do it: overpower the guards and then hope for extreme luck in getting to the docks and stealing a ship. It'd be impossible to take off from the warship's docks while it was at jump speed, which meant that

Critch needed to find a place to lie low until the ship dropped out of jump. The odds were stacked against him.

"Screw it," he muttered. He crawled over to the only part of the entire cell that wasn't smooth or curved, a support rod under his bunk that was screwed into the floor. It took some maneuvering to slide under the bunk and into position on the squared metal bracket that was between the rod and the floor. He had to assume they weren't watching him, or else his ploy would be blown before he even got through the door.

He grimaced. Then slammed his forehead into the edge. He saw bright white the instant before the pain hit him, followed by a warm trickle of blood. Red droplets made a sharp contrast on the white floor, and he pushed to his feet, letting the blood flow freely down his face in a trail.

He leaned an arm against the wall as he tapped the service button on the wall near the door. He pressed it three more times before someone answered. "What do you want?"

Still leaning against the wall, Critch looked up at the camera and pointed to his wound. "I hit my head when the ship jumped. I don't feel so good. I think I got a concussion." He wobbled on his feet, perhaps overacting a touch.

After a pause, the same voice said, "Stand away from the door."

He pushed off the wall and collapsed in a seated position on his bunk.

The door opened, and the guard stood there. He held out a bandage. "Here. Take it."

Critch tried to stand but fell back. "The whole room's spinning."

The young man frowned as he thought through his options. He stepped forward and unraveled the bandage. "You better not throw up on me."

Critch leapt to his feet and punched the guard's throat before the man had any time to react. Unable to breathe, the guard clawed at his throat. Critch grabbed the guard's head and smashed it against the wall, and the man dropped. The guard was going to die from his throat being crushed, and despite his reputation, Critch didn't want to prolong the young man's suffering. He knew a better man would've grappled with the guard, but Critch knew better than to fight someone half his age—and who had weapons and a comm on him.

He rolled the guard over and grabbed everything he could in the brief seconds he could afford before someone noticed the door open and the guard missing. A blaster, a stun stick, and a wrist comm made Critch feel less vulnerable, and he strode from the cell. The hallway, as he'd expected, was still empty, though he knew it wouldn't be for long. He looked left and then took off running to the right.

Blood blinded his left eye, and he wiped it as he sprinted down the hallway. Every second he was out in the open, his captors could see him. Only once he found his way into the engineering tunnels—the bones of the ship—did he have a chance at evading capture and coming up with a plan that didn't involve him getting killed.

He didn't find an access point in the brig hallway—that would be a stupid design decision—so Critch had to venture into another hallway. When he reached the door, he slapped on the guard's wrist comm and scanned it over the lock pad. The door clicked and opened, and he hurried through. At a glance, he counted at least four people, two couples in civilian clothes, chatting with each other. He didn't understand why they weren't wearing uniforms, but he kept his head down as he rushed by them.

"Oh, dear! You're bleeding," a woman called out. "Do you need any help?"

"No," he said, and added a "thanks" to sound a little more like a citizen would speak, though he knew his tactical clothes would raise doubt. He turned a corner and found the access point he'd been looking for. He used the wrist comm to unlock the nondescript service door in the wall and stepped into the cold air. Puffs of his breath formed little clouds before him.

The wrist comm still worked, which meant they hadn't found the guard yet. He tore off the wrist comm and dropped it by the door. It'd have a locator chip in it, and they'd be able to track where he'd used it. Now that he was inside the ship's guts, he had free rein of several kilometers of hiding places.

He ran down the narrow walkway, trying to put as much distance between himself and the door he'd used before the hunting parties were sent out to scour the ship. While the hallways were well lit, the area between the ship's hull and the hallways had only dim LEDs lighting the walkways. Along his left was the smooth wall and service doors that separated Critch from everyone else. Along his right were pipes and conduits, and beyond those was several-feet-thick gel insulation that protected the ship against the small pieces of debris that floated everywhere in Collective—and Alliance—space. A one-inch chunk of plastic could tear through a foot of metal but only a couple inches of the gel insulation.

The scenery didn't change as Critch ran, and he searched for a stairway. He found one next to a service door. He took the stairs and descended several levels until he was at the lowest level. The floor he emerged onto was wide, and he knew it spanned the length and width of the ship. The ceiling was just high enough for him to run along the walkway without crouching.

He sprinted until he couldn't get enough air and his legs burned. He slowed, then jumped over the railing and onto a conduit line. In the ship's belly, the lines were easily the diameter of three men, making it easier for him to crawl under the low ceiling now that he was off the walkway. He scanned the thick conduit and pipes, ignoring the obvious hiding places and instead moving toward a crevice between two conduits.

He settled between the cold metal and tried to relax, but his adrenaline and pounding heart made it hard. After several minutes, his body caught on and he felt his muscles mellow. Wet with sweat, icy pricks seeped into his skin. He'd have to find a warmer spot or else deal with the prospect of hypothermia. He went to sit up, but lights came on across the ship's belly.

He lay back down and stilled, as though in a tomb. They'd discovered the guard and knew Critch was in the hull, but they couldn't know where. Finding someone who didn't want to be found in the service areas that spanned the entire warship made finding a needle in a haystack a piece of cake.

Critch smiled before a shiver clenched his teeth. He was free from the cell. But he had no water and no food, was in below-freezing temperatures, and was about to have a dromadier army on his ass.

CHAPTER 19

CRAZY HEROICS

Alliance airspace, near Spate

THE COLONIZATION FLEET rested near one of Spate's eight moons. The area resembled a shipyard with the flurry of drones and transports coming to and leaving from the fleet, delivering the agreed supplies for the long journey ahead. The Alliance's first destroyer, the *New Liberty*, glistened in the distance as it stood watch like a stern mother standing between her children and whatever may dare approach uninvited.

Playan transports were in the process of docking at the seven largest ships, ready to unload nearly a thousand tons of carbon fiber to be used to build new colonies in some far-off system.

Every transport carried carbon fiber and Tulan Port personnel, except for the *Henry Fitzroy*, which brought several additional passengers whose jobs were far different from those unloading supplies. Reyne, the leader of that group, rode in the cockpit along with the ship's captain as he docked with the *Littorio*.

As soon as the docking sequence was complete, Reyne unhooked his seatbelt and stood. "I appreciate the lift, Will."

"I'm happy to help. If things go south and you need help in there—"

"If things go south, I need you here and ready to take off in case we have to make a hasty departure."

Will gave a small nod. "I'll be here." He took a quick breath before continuing. "You're doing the right thing. It's what she would've done."

Reyne didn't need to ask which "she" Will had been referring to. Prior to flying the *Henry Fitzroy*, Will had piloted the *Arcadia* under the command of Gabriela Heid. Reyne smiled and tilted his head in Will's direction, then left the bridge.

In the hallway, he met with the rescue team: Sixx and Boden from his crew; Hari; Miko and Roq from the *Ocelot*; and Domino, Sadie, and Tracks from the *Lady Lilith*. All the specters were in orbit around Darios, waiting for a call to attack the *Littorio* if it came to that. Reyne sure hoped it wouldn't.

The rescue team wore tech coveralls over their usual garb to blend in with the large numbers of personnel unloading and moving supplies around the ship. The Playan crew went about unloading the shipment, and the rescue team wheeled one stack of pallets on board the warship.

Reyne looked around the bay, empty except for two techs logging the supplies.

Sixx frowned. "There're no droms. Why are there no droms?"

Reyne shrugged. "Maybe they don't have enough to cover all the docks. Maybe they have something else on their hands. Maybe they trust us colonists."

Sixx guffawed. "It's definitely not that last bit."

"With how lax the security is, I bet we could walk this ship end to end without anyone even noticing," Boden said.

"Let's hope it stays that way. It'd make our job a whole lot easier." Reyne inhaled and rubbed his hands together. "Okay, this is where we part ways for now. Now, let's see if these techs are fans of Marshal Aramis Reyne. Either way, you can count on me to keep these guys busy while you bring our boy back."

With that, Reyne left the team and strode over to the techs. "Hi, I'm—"

"Aramis Reyne," one of the techs interrupted. "You're the torrent marshal. You led the Battle of Sol Base."

"I did, but I hope we can be friends now that the war is over."

The tech waved a hand through the air. "I always thought war was a stupid idea. You guys should've been free ages ago. Just about everyone on Alluvia thought so."

"It's true," the other tech said. "I thought it was cool to see colonists really stand up for themselves for once."

"Well, thanks, I guess," Reyne said, and flashed a smile at his departing teams. With all the risks this rescue mission had, they deserved one thing to go right.

"I never thought I'd meet you in person, especially with leaving on this mission so soon. What can I do for you?" the first tech asked.

"As my people are busy moving the carbon fiber on board, I was hoping you could tell me more about this big trip you've got planned. I've been considering joining your fleet."

"Really?" the first tech said. "We have plenty of room on all the ships. I mean, take the *Littorio*, for example. She's running on only fifteen percent of the recommended crew size. That's even less than a skeleton crew."

"Not a lot of people are ready to give up everything to fly into the unknown for what could be the rest of their lifetimes. As for me, I had nothing to lose. I get a private cabin that's bigger than my apartment back on Alluvia," the second tech added.

The first tech spoke again. "I heard that the whole colonization idea started over a year ago—"

"He doesn't want to know the story. He wants to learn about the mission," the other tech butted in, and turned to Reyne. "This mission is bigger than anything that's ever been done before. Not only will we be leaving the system, but we'll also be going beyond what there are jump charts for. It's going to be incredible. Let me tell you all about it..."

"Let's go," Sixx said quietly as the techs became completely absorbed in their conversation with the famous torrent marshal-turned-stationmaster.

The group of eight, all carrying toolboxes containing their weapons and specialty gear, casually strode from the bay and into the first hallway. Sixx paused. "Okay team, now that we're on board, check your comms to make sure Critch's tracker is still displaying, along with all our locations. I'm showing he's just about directly below us, fourteen levels down." When everyone verified, he continued. "It's time to go into position. Miko and Roq, you cover the *Henry Fitzroy*. Domino, Sadie, and Tracks, cover any access point to this landing bay. Hari and Boden, you're with me to grab Critch. Don't shoot anyone unless your cover is blown, got it?"

"I still think we should have the specters hit Alluvia and Myr while the armada is out chasing after their lost fleet. Then they'd hand over Critch without question," Tracks said.

"Let's try to accomplish this mission without starting another war. Now, keep your heads in the game and get where you need to be," Sixx said, and added under his breath, "Dumbass."

As soon as Sixx had met the specters—Critch's pirate army turned torrent army—he knew they were a shoot-first-ask-questions-later sort of team. He'd warned Reyne against taking them along on a mission where shooting was a last resort, but Reyne had stood firm that they needed all the help they could get to extricate Critch. Sixx didn't tell him that if they found themselves in a gunfight, Critch and all of them would likely be dead and the extra help wouldn't make any difference.

He was glad Bree had stayed back. That woman constantly surprised him. She was one hell of a fighter, but she also had a better head on her shoulders than Sixx. She knew Sixx would've refused to stay behind, and so she'd chosen to stay without their usual rock-paper-scissors game to decide who went. He hadn't thought he could care for someone as much as he had for Qelle. He'd been wrong. He now cared for not one, but two who made his heart full—and ache any time he was forced to leave them behind.

At least, if something happened to him on this mission, Lily would have someone she loved to take care of her. Once he returned to Nova Colony, he'd tell Bree and Lily that he wouldn't take any more missions without them, which meant he wouldn't take any more dangerous missions. Bree and Lily deserved better, and he wanted the chance to see what having a family was really all about.

Sixx refocused on the mission and scanned the hallway for an elevator. As the three teams parted ways, he headed his team to the nearest elevator down the hall on his left.

In their short walk, they came across only one tech, and she didn't even look up from her tablet.

Hari glanced over her shoulder before speaking, to make sure the tech hadn't stopped. "The brig on the *Littorio* is located on level Eight. That's *above* us."

Sixx nodded, as he had also studied the warship's layout beforehand and knew the brig had been their greatest risk. "Good thing he's showing below us then."

"But why isn't he in the brig? His tracker's still online, so he's still alive," Boden said.

Hari's lips curled upward. "It's Critch. I bet he broke out."

"All that matters to us is that he's alive and below us. We can philosophize on the whys later," Sixx said.

He stopped at the elevator, took in a breath, and pressed the lowest floor listed on the touchscreen. The screen flashed INSUFFICIENT AUTHORITY.

"The lowest level is always a service area," Boden said. "Someone with either tech or security authority should be able to get us in there."

"Then we'll find someone," Sixx said as he pressed the second lowest floor. The elevator opened to reveal two droms in full armor and carrying rifles.

The three stepped inside and stood in front of the droms.

Sixx turned around and eyed the female soldier, who noticed and cocked her head at him. He nodded to her gear. "Aren't you guys a bit overdressed?"

"We're just running some drills. Nothing for you to worry about," she replied.

He gave his smile, the one that had worked magic on many women—and a good number of men—through the years. "I'm not worried. That armor fits you nicely."

Her features softened, and he knew he had her.

"Hey, maybe you can help us," Sixx continued. "We're rilon techs from Tulan Port. Stationmaster Reyne assigned us to the lowest deck to repair a busted magnetron liner, but we can't seem to get to it from here."

"Oh, that's because you need authority access," she replied. "They should've assigned an onboard tech to escort you."

Sixx frowned. "I was wondering about that. Is there any way you could escort us? It shouldn't take long. We've already been given a map and the area we need to check out."

"Well, we're still on duty, but—"

"We can't help you. We're busy running drills," the other soldier blurted, and shot a hard look at his partner.

"But it'd be safe. There are plenty of us in the service areas," she said.

"We can't. We're in the middle of drills," he said.

"Oh, I see," Sixx said, not believing for a moment that they were involved with drills of any sort. He made an obvious show of reading their name badges. "Well, thanks anyway, Wilton and Rodriguez. Since Stationmaster Reyne is on board, I'll call him and—"

"The stationmaster is on board?" the male drom asked.

"Yeah. He's overseeing the delivery, and I think he was going to meet with the Corps General. So, when they meet, they should be able to get this worked out. Don't worry, I'll be sure to mention your names and that you would've helped if you could."

The droms glanced at each other. The elevator stopped and opened on their floor. All five moved, but then the pair squeezed around the three.

"I suppose it wouldn't hurt to give you access to get your work done," the female drom said.

The male scanned his wrist comm and selected the lowest level. "There. No need to bother the Corps General. Just be sure not to waste any time down there."

"Believe me, we won't. We'll take care of what we need and get out of there. You have my word," Sixx said with a smile.

The elevator closed, sealing off the three from the soldiers.

"Well, that was convenient," Hari said.

"That's Sixx's way," Boden added.

"And no one got shot," Sixx tacked on.

"We'll have to be careful. They said there were droms down there already," Boden said.

"I'm thinking Hari was right," Sixx said. "Our wayward orphan broke himself out."

The elevator opened, and they stepped into the cold underbelly of the warship. The narrow walkway required them to stand in single file. They looked over the sea of massive pipes and storage tanks. Sixx glanced at his wrist comm to find the red dot at his two o'clock a couple hundred meters away. Then he looked to his left and to his right down the lengths of the walkway. In the far distance of each side stood droms. Unfortunately, the ones to their right were headed their way.

He exhaled, and his breath formed a cloud in the still air. He motioned to the pair. "Keep your game faces on." He turned right and led them down the walkway until the red dot was straight off his left. The pair of droms were within fifty meters of their position. Not wanting to give away any hint of Critch's location, Sixx walked past the dot and toward the droms.

The pair slowed as the distance between the groups closed.

"Hey, what are you doing down here? The service areas are off-limits during drills," one of the droms said as everyone came to a stop.

Sixx held up his hand. "Blame it on a magnetron for not waiting for your drills to finish to break."

"No one said there'd be tech down here," the other soldier said.

"We just want to do our jobs. Wilton and Rodriguez said it was okay," Sixx said.

The first guard who spoke rolled his eyes. "Fine. Whatever. Just be careful down here."

"Why?" Sixx asked.

The guards glanced at each other. "Just rumors that we might have a stowaway or two who snuck on board to join the trip. If you see anyone, call it in immediately. Do *not* approach him— them, I mean. They could be dangerous."

"Sure thing." Sixx said as they squeezed past one another on the walkway. "Thanks for keeping the ship safe."

Sixx, Boden, and Hari walked as slowly as they could without looking like they were biding time. Every now and then, one would point at something as though analyzing it for inspection. Sixx shivered. "I could think of quite a few better places to hang out than here."

"But no others provide as many hiding spots," Hari said.

Sixx glanced back to see the pair of droms standing by the elevator, watching them. He gritted his teeth. "Looks like we're not going to be able to wait them out. We're doing this with an audience." He grabbed the handrail to jump off the walkway.

"Wait," Boden said. "There are traction strips on that pipe over there. Techs would be trained to walk along those pipes for safety."

"Oh. Right. How about you lead the way?"

Boden backtracked them to the nearby pipe and opened a gate in the rail Sixx hadn't noticed. He stepped out on to the huge pipe. Hari followed, and Sixx covered their backs. He didn't turn to see if the droms were watching—he knew they were.

Despite being the largest of the trio, Boden moved with the most grace over the somewhat curved surface. Sixx realized Boden was used to moving through uneven spaces, given he was a ship mechanic.

Boden stopped at a pipe that ran perpendicular to and above the larger pipe they'd walked on. He grabbed the ladder that ran down the side and climbed up. Hari and Sixx followed, and Boden led them to the next ladder. They then climbed down onto a parallel pipe even lower than the first one they'd taken, cutting off the view from the walkway and, more importantly, the droms.

Boden stared at his wrist comm for a moment before looking up and walking briskly toward Critch's beacon. Hari and Sixx followed, helping each other at the occasional slip on the smooth surface.

The mechanic slowed, stopped, and did a three-sixty. "I don't understand. He should be right here."

Hari and Sixx joined him in searching the immediate area. They looked above, below, and everywhere around them.

"Critch?" Sixx called out, keeping the word barely above a whisper.

"Hold on," Hari said. She leapt to a smaller pipe running alongside theirs. She sat, straddling the pipe, and looked over the outer side, then slid down and disappeared. "I found him. Get over here."

Sixx and Boden leapt and slid smoothly off the pipe to find Hari kneeling next to a body wedged between the ship's gel insulation and the pipe they'd slid down. Sixx turned to Boden. "Cover us."

Boden nodded and pulled guns from his toolbox.

"He's alive, but not responsive," she said, worry quickening her words. "He doesn't have his wrist comm, so I can't see his bioscans. Other than a superficial cut on his forehead, I don't see any signs of injury."

"He's alive. Nothing else matters until we get him out of here and back to our ship," Sixx said. He looked over Hari's shoulder at Critch's unconscious form. Blue lips, pale skin, sunken eyes... the man looked like a corpse already.

Sixx bent down, opened his toolbox and pulled out the first aid kit. "Here."

Hari looked back. He handed her a shot and the three electrolyte vials he had. She tried a couple times with the syringe before finding a vein. She inserted the first vial. Sixx watched as it drained.

"How'd you see him?" he asked.

"I didn't. I smelled him."

Critch was so wedged into the insulation, likely for warmth, that it was also blocking the worst of his odor. Now that Sixx was practically on top of the other man, he admitted that Critch wasn't the worst thing he'd ever smelled—after all, Sixx had grown up in Devil Town—but Critch damn near topped the list.

"He's so dehydrated, the cold is probably the only reason he's still alive."

After she finished administering the three vials, Sixx handed her a chem boost.

She held the nasal spray under Critch's nose and squeezed. His eyes shot open, only to fall back closed.

Hari ran a hand through Critch's hair with a gentleness Sixx had never seen in her before. "Stay with me." She turned to Sixx. "I don't suppose you brought something for hypothermia."

Sixx shook his head. "We'll get him in a tank as soon as possible."

"Hurry. The droms are walking out on the pipes," Boden said in a low voice.

"Distract them if you have to," Sixx muttered back. "It's going to take a while to get him out of here."

Boden grumbled something, and Sixx heard fading footsteps on the pipe above them.

They tugged Critch free, and both embraced him to feed him their body heat. Sixx grimaced and changed his mind: Critch topped his list.

"He must've been down here for the better part of a week. Being a soft-freeze ice cream cone is definitely what kept him alive," he said. "Just like usual, Critch is screwing up our plans. I was counting on him walking out with us. There's no way we can sneak off this ship while carrying him."

"Would a carbon fiber box hold him?"

"Maybe. If we can manage to get one down here and back up to the ship without anyone the wiser."

Critch groaned.

She shook her head. "That could take hours. He doesn't have that kind of time."

Sixx grabbed two handguns and a rifle from the toolbox and pushed it to the side. "Sounds like we're going with Plan B."

She grimaced and went for her weapons. She pulled out a pair of coveralls and hat that matched their outfits, glanced at Critch, then tossed them aside. "I was afraid you were going to say that."

After holstering his blasters and slinging the rifle over his shoulder, Sixx typed out a single letter "B" and sent it to the rescue team, Reyne, and Will.

A moment later, hurried footsteps approached. "We're going to Plan B?" Boden asked.

"Yep," Sixx said as he hefted Critch up. "Help pull him up."

Boden grabbed the limp man under his arms and pulled while Sixx pushed.

"Hey! What's taking you so long back there?" a voice yelled out.

"Fixing a magnetron liner isn't just slapping a patch on it," Sixx yelled back.

Boden set Critch down on the pipe. "Magnetrons don't have liners."

Sixx climbed up and pulled out his guns and from his toolbox. "That's nice."

"You don't even know what a magnetron is, do you?" Boden asked.

"Not a clue." Sixx peeked through the pipes and saw two pairs of boots less than fifty meters from them. He spun around to face Boden and Hari. "Hari, you get us to that elevator as fast as you can. Boden and I will keep up with Critch. Ready for some fun times?"

"Where are you at? Come out now," the same voice yelled.

Hari gave a single nod and headed down the pipe in the opposite direction to the one they'd arrived from, away from the pair of droms. The pipe was smaller than the higher pipes, and Sixx and Boden had to carry Critch between them as they ran sideways, with Boden in lead. Sixx struggled to keep up.

"We're on a straight path to the elevator," Hari said. "We have to climb up and go visible. I'll lay down cover fire."

Hari climbed the metal rungs up the pipe.

Boden and Sixx struggled hauling Critch up the short ladder. With every upward movement, Critch made a small sound.

Once they reached the pipe, the width of this pipe allowed them to jog side by side with Critch between them. Their passenger moaned at being jostled.

"Hang in there, you old pirate," Sixx said.

"There they are! Wait. They have the target!"

Sixx didn't turn to locate the droms; instead, he ran faster. Shots were fired, and a pipe near Sixx's head suddenly had a blackened hole in it.

Hari laid down a barrage of rifle fire.

The elevator was fewer than fifteen meters away. Hari sprinted ahead and reached the walkway. She lunged at the elevator and punched the level for the docking bays. Then she spun around, got down on a knee, and scanned the area through her rifle scope, firing off shots into the piping as well as at the walkway to their right.

Gunfire came at them from at least two directions, but Sixx had no hand free to fire. All he could do was hope the droms were far enough away that they couldn't get direct hits. Boden climbed over the railing, then dragged Critch over. Sixx jumped over without pause.

Two droms were on the walkway, sprinting toward them, but Hari was busy holding off the pair just leaving the pipe on their left.

Sixx kept one arm around Critch's waist while he unslung his rifle. He aimed it at the pair running toward him. They were firing, but their gait was screwing up their aim and their shots were all over the place. Sixx took his time and fired. *One. Two.* Two shots fired; two headshots.

The elevator chimed, and they bunched up to get in. The door opened, and they came face to face with two more droms. Everyone raised their weapons simultaneously. Sixx felt pressure in his side, like someone snapped a rubber band on his skin. He ignored it and fired his rifle at the drom's face. At near point blank, it was messy but effective. The other drom was already down, dropped by either Hari or Boden. They jumped in over the bodies and held their rifles at the opening. When the door closed, the trio let out a collective sigh.

Sixx's side began to burn—a sensation he was no stranger to—and he gritted his teeth.

Boden slapped a yellow button on the wall. The screen above it read PRESS HERE FOR EXPRESS LIFT. NOTE: USE ONLY FOR EMERGENCIES.

"This classifies as an emergency," Boden said as he tapped the screen. "That should get us to our floor without more interruptions. Well, unless they stop us from the control room." He noticed Hari rubbing her ribs where a black hole now showed on her coveralls. "You're shot."

"I got lucky. It didn't get through my chest plate. Did Critch get shot?"

"He's clear," Sixx said, and touched his side. He pulled his fingers away to find them warm and wet with blood. "I didn't get so lucky."

Boden gave him a concerned look. "How bad?"

"Just a graze," Sixx said.

Boden gave him that Boden-esque condescending look that

made it clear the man thought Sixx was lying, but he didn't voice his thoughts.

Hari stepped closer. "Here. At least let me take Critch."

Sixx wanted to argue, but the truth was that he'd lied. He had maybe an hour before he needed to be in front of a doctor. He wasn't so much of an idiot that he'd burn through his last remaining energy carrying Critch when Hari was capable.

He released Critch, and Hari moved in smoothly to grab him.

The man moaned and wobbled his head. "...feel like shit." The words sounded like his tongue didn't work.

"You smell like it, too, but we still decided to take you along," Sixx said while keeping his rifle on the door.

Shivers coursed over Critch, and he whimpered.

Hari cupped his face in her free hand and kissed him on the cheek. "Hang in there. We're almost out."

Sixx frowned. "Wait. You—and him? You two?"

She shot him a hard look, and he thought better than to continue that line of questioning.

The elevator stopped.

Sixx noticed the floor. They were one level below the docking bay.

"Well, *shit.*"

CHAPTER 20

PLAN B

On board the Littorio, *in Alliance airspace*

AS SOON AS Reyne saw the letter "B" flash across his wrist comm, his stomach dropped. He'd hoped they could've done it quietly, but the odds had been heavily stacked against them for a retrieval that didn't include a body count.

"It looks like I have a call I need to take, so if you'll excuse me, I'd better be going," Reyne said to the two techs he'd been keeping busy and away from the *Henry Fitzroy.*

He took off before they could respond, and walked as briskly as he could toward the docking bay. As he walked, he notified the specters to make way toward the colonization fleet. Plan B meant all bets were off. If they needed a space battle to get off this warship, they'd get one.

He met Miko and Roq on the way, and they joined him, rifles ready. At the far end of the hallway, on the other side of the bay, he saw Domino, Sadie, and Tracks, also carrying rifles. Reyne unholstered his handgun. Unlike the rest of the techs and the rescue team, a stationmaster had no problem carrying a gun wherever he damn well chose.

He glanced at his wrist comm regularly to make sure the dots for Sixx, Boden, Hari, and now Critch were making progress toward the docking bay.

Reyne's team closed in on the elevator that held their friends. On arrival, at least one full squad of droms was shooting at them from a position around a corner. Unable to see the droms, Reyne backed up to the touchpad, trying to make himself as small as possible. "Hold this position," he yelled at his team.

The team spread out against the wall, a couple of the team members going down on a knee.

"We're sitting ducks out here," Domino yelled as she fired back.

"They're almost to us," Reyne yelled back.

Fortunately, the droms around the corner were firing blind and their shots sprayed down the hallway, landing far down from the team's position.

Reyne glanced at his wrist comm to see what was taking the other team so long. The elevator had stopped a floor below them. His jaw clenched. "Nothing's ever easy around here," he muttered. Then he spoke up. "Looks like we have to go bring our friends back."

He looked across the hallway to the nearest stairwell. He tapped Domino's shoulder and nodded to her two crew members. "You three with me. Miko, Roq, keep this stairwell open for us."

Reyne took a breath, covered his head, then leapt across the hallway and slammed into the far wall. He pressed the button to open the door and jumped to the side. When no gunfire came out, he entered the stairwell. Unlike the elevator, and due to the fire code, doors to the stairwells didn't have locks. That fact was both a help and a hindrance.

Domino, Sadie, and Tracks followed him into the stairwell. Domino raised her rifle to scan the stairs above them while Sadie leaned over the railing and scanned below. Reyne led the way down the winding dozen or so steps.

The door was closed on the next level, which meant that as soon as Reyne hit the button, the door would automatically open and they'd lose any element of surprise. But he expected someone in a control room to have the stairs on a vid feed already. He turned to face his group. "Any of you have a smoke or maybe a shock grenade?"

"I have a whole line of regular grenades," Tracks said. He grinned, showing teeth grayed by years of too much Blue Tea, and opened his coveralls to reveal at least six grenades looped on his vest.

Domino shrugged. "My crew only uses the real things, too."

Reyne glanced at his comm to see four dots bundled together on the other side of the door. "Can't use those. Maybe next time."

"I have a few gas pellets," Sadie said. "It'll give them vertigo for a good ten seconds."

"I don't have a mask," Reyne said.

"Neither do I," said Sadie. "I usually just toss them into a room and count to three."

Reyne nodded. "Sounds good. I'll open the door, you toss the pellets, and I'll close the door."

He went to open the door. "Wait. Is that ten seconds after your three-count or including it?"

She looked up as she thought. "After, I think."

"Okay. We move fast." He waited until she held the pellets and nodded. Then he pressed the button. The door opened with a swish, Sadie flung the pellets, and Reyne smacked the button again. For a split-second while the door was open, Reyne saw the hallway. There seemed to be twenty droms around their small group, who were kneeling in the middle. Hari and Boden held Critch, whose body was slumped over.

"...two and one. Go!" Sadie said.

Ten. Reyne took a breath, hit the button for a third time, and lunged into the hallway. Any gas had already dissipated, and the droms nearest his people were leaning on each other or the walls.

Nine.

He knocked over a few getting to his people, who were just as wobbly on their hands and knees.

Eight.

Several droms outside the main group didn't seem to be affected. They aimed their rifles at Reyne and his team, but didn't fire. Reyne grabbed the nearest drom to use as a shield.

Seven.

"Surrender," one of them yelled.

Reyne dragged the drom with him. He noticed Domino had done the same.

Six.

They released their shields at the same time to grab the first two of their people. Reyne grabbed Critch, and found he had to bear the full weight of the man.

Five.

He grunted and hefted Critch through the crowd of dizzy droms, Domino right behind with Hari. He was making a big assumption that the droms wouldn't fire into their own people. If he was wrong, he wouldn't be alive to learn from it, anyway.

Four.

Sadie pushed by to grab Sixx. Reyne noticed she was struggling with him. Tracks had Boden, who seemed to be the least wobbly.

Everyone was nearly recovered.

Three. Damn it.

The three-count was included in the ten seconds. Reyne opened the door and jumped through. Critch moaned but didn't otherwise show any hints of consciousness.

"Stop them!"

Domino brought Hari, who stepped away to stand on her own. "I'm good," she said as she grabbed her rifle. Reyne stood by the button to close the door, but knew he hadn't really thought that part through, since the droms could open it any time they wanted.

Sadie stepped through with Sixx, only to have a drom grab her shoulder and yank her back. Sixx tumbled through and leaned against the wall, holding his side.

Hari leapt forward and fired into the hallway. At least one soldier went down. The others scattered. She held out a hand and pulled Sadie through.

Tracks let go of Boden as they reached the doorway. As Boden stepped through, Reyne noticed too late that Hari's gunfire had cleared the area, opening up his team to the droms down the hallway. Tracks was just about through the doorway when red spray painted the wall. Tracks grabbed his neck, but it was impossible to stop the arterial blood from spurting.

Domino raced forward to grab Tracks, but Tracks grimaced and stepped back into the hallway. He reached inside his coveralls.

"Don't move!" a drom yelled.

As the soldiers closed in, Tracks smiled and pulled out a grenade.

Reyne slammed the button. The door closed an instant before the explosion shook the stairwell. The door bowed inward.

Boden jumped over and helped carry Critch while Domino and Sadie grabbed Sixx. With Hari leading the way, they ran up the stairs as quickly as they could. At the top, Hari took a deep breath as her hand froze over the door's button. "Here goes nothing." She hit the button and swung her rifle up before the door had fully opened.

Another battle was taking place. Hari peeked around the doorway for less than a second before backing up. "Looks like four droms to our left at twenty meters. Miko and Roq are covering the door to our landing bay seventy meters to our right. Miko is down, and Roq is holding them off."

"We're lucky they're running on a skeleton crew. If this was a fully staffed warship, we'd have a couple thousand droms coming out of the woodwork," Reyne said.

Sadie released Sixx and stepped forward. She pulled out a grenade. "For Tracks," she said and hurled it down the hallway to her left. She casually regained her hold on Sixx, who was paler than Reyne had ever seen him.

An explosion boomed. Hari glanced back out in the hallway.

"It's clear! Get your asses out here! I think you busted my eardrums!" came Roq's mousy voice.

Reyne didn't bother checking. He and Boden rushed out, dragging Critch and moving in that unrhythmic way one does when carrying bags that are too heavy. He trusted the others were behind. Roq struggled to lift Miko as they approached. Hari ran around Reyne and helped Roq, and the two women hefted the unconscious larger man between them.

The door to their docking bay was held open with a crowbar. Miko's feet dragged over the bar, nearly knocking it away. Reyne winced and grabbed the door. Fortunately the bar held, and Reyne and Boden gingerly carried Critch through. They ran forward through the pressurization chamber that enveloped the ramp of the box-shaped *Henry Fitzroy,* which at that moment was the most beautiful ship Reyne had ever seen.

Several Tulan Port techs stood at the top of the ramp, slack-jawed and wide-eyed.

Reyne spoke. "You want to make some hazard pay, help get these injured on board and to some beds."

They didn't need to be told twice. Five rushed down the ramp and relieved Reyne and Boden of Critch's body and Hari and Roq of Miko's. Domino and Sadie continued on board with Sixx. Reyne checked on his friend as they went by.

Sixx's eyes were glazed, but he was able to make eye contact.

"You doing okay?" Reyne asked, not knowing the right way to ask his friend how badly he was injured.

"I'll be fine in no time," he said, and winced as a tech tried to assist. Domino stepped back to let the tech relieve her.

The clang of metal brought Reyne's attention to the door, where Boden had kicked out the crowbar.

"Let's get on board," Reyne said.

A tech came running to him. "We can't leave. The captain said they've locked the ship. He can't override it."

A big ol' rock suddenly weighed heavily in Reyne's gut. "Of course they locked us in."

"I can override it," Boden said.

Relief flooded Reyne. "Good. Then let's get you on the bridge."

Boden shook his head. "The manual override is in the docking bay."

"Absolutely not," Reyne snapped back. "We'll find another way. We always do."

Boden swallowed. "Not this time. And you know the droms will be here any time now."

Reyne stood, staring at his friend.

"Get on board and tell Will to be ready. You won't have much of a window."

Reyne, still mute, took a couple steps and embraced Boden. When he stepped back, he found words. "If they let you surrender, you damn well better surrender. We'll come for you, just like we came for Critch."

Boden gave him a weak smile.

"Hey, Bodie," Domino said from behind Reyne.

Boden looked up in time to catch a grenade.

She shrugged. "Just in case."

He gave a quick nod, then turned and ran back into the docking bay. He picked up the crowbar and held it in one hand and the grenade in the other. He strode toward a control panel on the wall while the sound of blaster shots came through the door from the hallway, and pried the panel open with the crowbar.

Domino grabbed Reyne by the arm and tugged him on to the ship. "We need to close the ramp door."

He allowed her to lead him on board, but stood just inside the door and kept his eyes on Boden until the door closed him off. When that happened, he rushed to the bridge, where he could keep tabs on what was taking place in the docking bay.

Will was in the captain's seat, his fingers flying over the instruments.

"How're we looking?" Reyne asked as he claimed a seat.

"As long they have those locks on us, we're not going anywhere," Will said.

"Just be ready. He'll get them off," Reyne said, and believed his words.

The view screen was designed for panoramic views of space, not close video, causing a grainy landing bay scene on the other side of the massive clear pane that separated the pressurized ship from space. Still, Reyne watched as Boden worked through the mess of wires in the control panel. Then he abruptly stepped back and looked at the ship.

"He did it! The locks are detaching now," Will said. He applied power too soon, and the ship groaned against the locks before being propelled backward when the last of the locking mechanisms released.

Boden waved, and Reyne lifted his arm, even though the mechanic couldn't see inside the ship. Boden's form became smaller and smaller as the ship backed out of the bay, until Reyne could no longer make out his shape. A second later, a bright orange-yellow explosion caused Reyne to shield his eyes.

When he looked again, the docking bay they'd been in was gone, and air and debris were venting into space. He scanned the debris for Boden but couldn't find any trace. His crew member was gone.

He collapsed against the back of his chair.

"We're not out of the woods yet," Will said.

Reyne forced himself to face the captain.

"There's nothing stopping the *Littorio* from shooting us into the abyss. She keeps hailing us, but I plan to keep ignoring her."

"Where are the specters?" Reyne asked.

"Still en route. They're not close enough to attack the fleet yet. Oh, crap."

"What is it?"

"The *New Liberty* has fired up her engines and is now moving toward the fleet. If she stays on course, we'll be sand-wiched between a warship and a destroyer," Will said.

"Change course," Reyne said, "and prepare to jump as soon as you have a clearing."

"Don't change course."

Reyne snapped around to see Hari jog on to the bridge.

She pointed at the destroyer growing larger on the view screen. "Head straight for the *New Liberty*."

Reyne frowned. "Are you crazy?"

"No," she said with a steady voice. "We have three passengers who need immediate medical attention. They won't survive the jump to Nova Colony."

"But who's to say the *New Liberty* won't shoot at us or ship us back to the *Littorio*?"

She cocked her head at him. "You really thought Seda wouldn't help us out? He'd never sell out his friends. Fields is out there to protect *us*, not the colonization fleet."

Reyne thought for a moment before chuckling. "Damn. Now I owe that politician an apology."

CHAPTER 21

CHANGES IN SEASONS

On board the New Liberty

"BUT YOU SAID you thought scars were sexy," Sixx whined.

Bree scowled at him. "Scars are, not corpses. If that blaster shot was one inch higher—"

"Good thing it wasn't, huh?" Sixx smiled.

"Can I see it, Dad?" Lily asked.

"Sure," Sixx said, caught Bree's disapproving look, and added, "when the bandage comes off."

Lily crossed her arms over her chest and pouted. "I've seen worse, you know."

Sixx's features tightened. "I know, Snookum."

Bree wrapped an arm around the girl. She and Sixx shared a knowing glance, then she spoke. "Lily, there's been something we've been wanting to talk to you about."

"Is it about Simon?"

Bree flinched. "How did you know?"

The eight-year-old rolled her eyes. "You two aren't very quiet when you whisper."

Sixx cocked his head. "What'd we tell you about eaves-dropping?"

She shrugged. "Well, it should be okay if it's about me."

"It's not okay, anytime," Bree said.

"Unless you're getting paid to do it," Sixx said with a wide grin. Lily laughed. Bree nudged him, and he grimaced.

Lily sobered. "Don't make me go live with Simon. I want to be with you." Tears welled up in her eyes. "If you don't want me anymore, I can go away, but please don't make me go with him."

Bree embraced the girl, and Sixx reached out and held her as best he could while confined in the hospital bed.

"We love you and never, ever want you to go away. Not ever," Bree said.

Lily sniffled.

"You're my daughter," Sixx said. "I will do everything in the galaxy to keep you safe. If you want me to make sure that Simon Tate never comes after you, I can make sure of that."

A small smile formed. "You'd shoot him for me?"

"You bet, Snookum."

Bree's lips thinned. "Sixx, remember how we talked about being good parental examples."

"Maybe just in the foot, then," Sixx offered.

Lily's smile broadened.

"Do you like Nova Colony?" Sixx asked Lily. "That's one place Simon can't go."

She nodded. "It's warmer than Playa. And I like playing in the tunnels."

"Ah, so we've got ourselves a tunnel rat," Sixx said.

Lily showed her two front teeth and held up clawed hands, mimicking a rodent scurrying around.

"Then Nova Colony it is," Bree said. She furrowed her brow and turned to Sixx. "But Reyne—"

"Will understand," Sixx said. "He'd want me to live with my wife and daughter."

Her frown deepened. "But—"

Sixx smiled. "Why not make it official? We could get married and adopt Lily—I mean, at least the adoption would be legal in the Alliance, even if the Collective ignores it."

Bree raised a brow. "Is that your idea of a marriage proposal? Because if it is, that's got to be the worst one ever."

"We're going to be a real family, not just a make-believe family?" Lily asked, her eyes wide.

Sixx looked to the girl. "Oh, Snookum, we're already a real family. But yeah, we'll be a real, *real* family."

Reyne stood next to Sixx, who sat in a wheelchair, Bree and Lily to his right. He found it hard to believe that just a few years ago he'd had four crew members, all of whom had been with him for over fifteen years. First to be lost was Doc. Then Throttle left for a new adventure, though he'd been expecting her to leave the nest for a long time. And now Boden.

Only Sixx remained, and he'd just informed Reyne that he and Bree were moving to Nova Colony, where Lily would be safe. Rather than disappointed, Reyne was happy to see Sixx move forward with his life. His friend had spent far too many years stuck in the past, searching for a long-lost wife, and letting vengeance fill his heart. While Reyne would miss Sixx, he knew there was a season for everything. And the season of the *Gryphon* seemed to be coming to an end.

Reyne's bones ached with arthritis and more—years of bearing too many burdens had weighed him down. After five decades of action, he craved a break from rebellions and fighting. *Soon.*

He looked across to see Commander Fields standing before her small army of Alliance Marines. She had a strong presence—unafraid to make hard decisions, yet her humanity evident in the way she looked at people and spoke, as though every person were a family member. He had no doubt she'd make the finest military leader the Alliance would ever have. If the colonies had to face war again, he knew they'd be in good hands.

They didn't need him anymore.

Reyne glanced to his left to see Critch, also in a wheelchair. Hari stood by him, and Reyne thought how they made such an odd couple—she a stalwart soldier, he a reckless rebel—yet they made perfect sense together. Seda stood nearby, with Layla on his arm. Another odd couple: the Alliance's first president and a prostitute as his public companion. Beyond them stood the remaining specter crews, nearly forty in all.

Between the Marines and the civilians stood two tubes. One bore the flag with a half lion, half eagle on it that matched the image painted on the side of the *Gryphon*. The other tube bore the flag with a naked woman covered only by a black cape—the *Lady Lilith*'s nose art. Domino, the *Lilith*'s captain, stood before Track's empty tube, giving his eulogy.

Boden's tube was empty, too, of course, but it didn't make the funeral any less meaningful. The two men had sacrificed themselves valiantly, without a second thought, to save their comrades. They were heroes, plain and simple.

Domino looked at Reyne, then stepped away. Reyne swallowed, took a breath, and trudged out to stand before Boden's casket. He looked around the hall one final time, seeing all the those assembled. Boden had saved at least that many lives throughout his life.

"Most of you who are standing here today never got the chance to meet Tren Boden. He kept to himself most of the time, and for much of that time, he spent working under engines and on all the things that keep my ship afloat. He was a good man, and I'm honored to have the chance to tell you about him.

"I met Boden sixteen years ago when my daughter, Throttle, and I were finishing a mail run from the fringe on Alluvia. The jump engine had gone offline on the last jump, so I was already running behind schedule. The engine shop at the docks gave me a one-month wait and was going to charge me more than what I made in two years hauling cargo. You know, the typical stuff citizen companies did to us colonists. I was stuck. If I didn't get my jump engine fixed, I'd never make my mail runs in time, but I didn't have that kind of money. And so, I left Throttle to watch over the ship while I went for a drink, hoping I'd find some inspiration in a swig of rum but at least knowing booze would soothe my nerves.

"I was sitting at this dive bar in First City when I met Boden. He was still a kid back then—barely eighteen and less than a week out of school—walking up to each and every patron in that bar and offering to do damn near anything in exchange for a ride off Alluvia. As that kid made his rounds, he'd get shoved away and spit on, yet he kept trying. Something about his perseverance got me that day. Either that, or I just always had a weak spot for an underdog. I offered him a lift in exchange for him essentially doing whatever I asked him to do. I figured he could load and unload cargo, give the ship a good cleaning, that sort of thing.

"I didn't expect much from the kid. After all, his eyes were still glassy; he was coming down from a sweet soy high. He was an addict—just like nearly every other citizen born from tenured parents—using drugs to escape being poor in a rich person's world. Even though he'd be soon looking for his next hit, I wasn't overly bothered." Reyne shrugged. "I guess we all have weaknesses, and I thought it was good to know a man's problems right out of the gate.

"But wouldn't you know, that kid showed at the *Gryphon* less than an hour after I met him. He carried a single suitcase. I'll always remember the expression on his face." Reyne reached out and pressed his hand against the tub and smiled. "Boden carried so much hope with him that he didn't need anything else. He dropped that suitcase of his on his bunk and went straight to work. He cleaned every inch of that ship—shined her to better than new—within the first day. By then, the engine shop of course hadn't started working on my jump engine yet. Throttle continued to tinker with the engine, but like me, she never had the gift for mechanicals. Now, Boden was a different story. He'd only worked on fishing boat motors before, but that didn't stop him. Throttle found him the manuals, and he dove right into that jump engine. I shouldn't neglect to mention that he and Throttle hit it off a little *too* well, if you know what I mean." Reyne gave a wry chuckle. "But that's a story for another day.

"Boden worked day and night on that engine for over a week, and damned if I know how he did it, but that kid got the engine running better than ever. And he performed those small miracles time and again over the years. "That was the thing about Boden. His brain was always working. He thrived on figuring out the inner workings of things. I never had to directly work with an engine shop again. Boden joined my crew and never backed down from a challenge, no matter what harm it posed to him." Reyne grimaced and swallowed. "I guess that's why I'm standing here today and he's not.

Reyne inhaled a shaky breath. He looked down for a moment to regain his composure. "But that was his choice, and his choices were what made him who he was. You see, Tren Boden was a dichotomy. He may have started out a fisherman—like his parents —yet he ended up working in space, the farthest place from any fish. He was a citizen, yet he had a colonist's spirit of adventure and yearned to be in the fringe. Sure, he was an addict, but he acted selflessly—time and again—to save lives. He fought in the battle to reclaim Sol Base, even though he didn't have a lick of soldiering experience.

"Now, I'm not here to turn Tren Boden into a larger-than-life hero. He wasn't perfect by any means. None of us are. He fought against his addiction every day. He could be moody and downright temperamental. Perhaps his worst fault was that he flirted with my daughter." He smirked, then sobered. "Joking aside, Boden was like a son to me, a friend to everyone he met, and a whole lot of people are alive today because of him." Tears welled in Reyne's eyes and he took a second to collect himself. "I suppose you could say Tren Boden is a larger-than-life hero after all."

Tension left Reyne's body, and he suddenly felt finished in more ways than having just given an eulogy. He straightened, and headed back toward his group. As he walked back, he was surprised to see Critch rolling his wheelchair toward him. They met briefly, Critch gave Reyne a knowing look and a nod, then Critch continued to the tubes.

When Reyne returned to his place, Sixx squeezed his shoulder. Reyne reciprocated. He turned back to the caskets to find Critch had stopped his chair in front of the tubes. Critch reached behind his chair, grabbed a case that had been in the back pocket, set it on his lap, and opened it.

When he pulled out the instrument, Reyne inhaled sharply. He hadn't seen Critch play a fiddle since the first Uprising. After a particularly bloody battle of New Teton, Critch had burned his fiddle, and Reyne had never seen his friend play since. It was too bad, too, because as much as Critch's scars scared little kids, his music moved people's spirits.

Reyne didn't know where Critch had found this fiddle, but he handled it as gently and respectfully as he would a fragile blown-glass egg. Critch placed the fiddle in position, raised the bow, paused, and then played. The music started slow, then sped up. It was an old Irish tune from Earth he'd heard Critch play a hundred times—always at a funeral. Critch said he'd learned the song from his grandfather, who'd learned it from his grandfather, and so it'd been passed down for a thousand years.

The music softened before building in intensity, and tears welled in Reyne's eyes as it brought forth memories of Boden finally beating his addiction. The sounds faded, but he could hear the music still playing in his head. The weight he'd felt before had lessened somewhat.

Critch put the fiddle back in its case and wheeled back to where their group waited. Reyne looked down at him, made eye contact, and gave him a small nod at a job well done. They turned back to see Commander Fields walk over to the tubes, then press controls on her wrist comm. The tubes propelled down their railings into the missile bays and shot out from the ship.

Then it was over.

People mingled. Others left. Sixx squeezed Reyne's shoulder before he and his family walked away, following Lily on some new adventure. Hari spoke with Seda. Many of the specters all headed in the same direction, which Reyne assumed was the way to the bar.

Reyne stood still, not quite ready to let go of the moment. Critch hadn't moved either. After a length, Reyne looked down at Critch. "I didn't know you'd started playing again."

Critch shrugged. "I hadn't until today."

"Well, I'm glad you did. So where are you off to after this?"

"Don't know yet. That bastard Anders blew up the *Honorless*, so I'm thinking about riding along with the specters for a time."

Reyne cringed. "That sounds miserable. For them, I mean."

Critch grunted.

"How about a new ship of your own?"

"Nothing could replace the *Honorless*."

"I know that, but I happen to know of a very nice ship—I hear she's the best out there—that may be coming available within the week."

Critch narrowed his gaze. "What are you talking about?"

Reyne patted his friend's shoulder. "I think it's time for the *Gryphon* to take on a new captain. Some fresh blood would do her good."

Critch thought for a moment. "She'd be a good ship. She's not the *Honorless*, but she's got spunk."

"Of course, you'll have to find yourself a crew."

"A crew for what?" Hari asked as she approached the pair.

Critch smiled. "I think I can pull one together."

Reyne "Well then, she's yours. On one condition."

Critch raised a brow. "What's that?"

"You have to give me a lift back to Tulan Port."

"But I heard you gave up the stationmaster gig. What's left for you there?" Critch asked.

Reyne smiled. "I have a date..."

CHAPTER 22

FINDING MASON

On board the Littorio

SEDA FAULK STEPPED out of the docking bay and into a damaged hallway. He glanced at the burn marks on the walls and had no doubt in his mind that Barrett Anders wanted him to see the damage the rescue mission had caused to the *Littorio*. He'd left Hari back on the *New Liberty*, since she was now a likely wanted criminal in Anders's eyes. Instead, he'd brought a pair of Marines on loan from Commander Fields. He knew two Marines posed little danger to dozens of dromadiers, but both Hari and Shauna had insisted.

A pair of dromadiers led Seda and his escorts first through the hallway, then up several floors in an elevator with dried blood smeared on the back. Seda had to give Anders credit—the man knew how to get a point across.

When the droms approached a closed cabin door, they stepped aside and motioned for Seda. "The captain will see you now," one said.

Seda turned to the Marines with him. "Stay here." He turned and entered.

Inside, he found Barrett Anders sitting behind a large wood desk.

"Corps General, it's good to see you," Seda approached and held out his arm.

They clasped forearms, and Anders spoke. "President Faulk, it's been too long. Though, you no longer need to address me by Corps General, as I believe the Collective has disowned both me and its colonization fleet. Parliament believes I gave them a black eye, when in fact I gave them every opportunity to embrace and champion the change."

"Hopefully, when you return, their perspective will have changed," Seda said as he took a seat across from Anders. "I saw the damage on my walk up here. How's the *Littorio* doing with repairs?"

"All critical repairs have been made. We're still scheduled to fly out tomorrow, and will make the remaining repairs en route." He paused. "The damage was far less important than the loss of life. That's why I wanted Drake Fender executed for his crimes before I left this system. This week, I lost twenty-six good crew members and have another thirty-two wounded because of him."

Seda cocked his head. "Forgive my bluntness, but those lives are on you. No one would've died if you had just left Fender alone."

"No one may have died on my ship, but more will die. Violence and anarchy are all he knows. Mark my words. As long as he's out there, more lives will be lost."

"If he crosses a line, I give you my word, I'll take care of it," Seda said.

"I hope you will, as we both know he's still alive thanks to your help," Anders said as he looked at Seda from the corner of his eye.

"I do not know what you're talking about," Seda said with feigned confidence.

Anders waved a hand through the air. "Let's not talk of that man again. There's too much to finish before the fleet jumps tomorrow and not nearly enough time."

"I agree," said Seda. "All the supplies have been transferred, and I've verified the credits have been deposited, so you should be covered there."

"Yes, yes, that's all good, but you know I like to get straight to the point," Anders said. "I wanted to talk with you about the future of the Founders."

"Ah, I see."

"Nearly every Founder has joined the colonization fleet. If the Founders aren't rebuilt, there's no one to guide the Collective —and now the Alliance, of course—in a way that represents *all* people, not just those in power."

Lately, the Founders had done far more damage than they'd ever done good. Seda and Hari had debated about whether the Founders still provided value or if they were simply an echo of a once-great organization. Seda didn't voice his thoughts. Instead, he said, "Continue."

"We need a leader to guide a new group of Founders, a group capable of empowering both the Collective and Alliance." Anders leaned forward. "I'm asking you to take on the mantel of Mason."

Seda carefully considered his response. "The Founders have had enough Masons already. Rather, fresh blood requires a fresh way of thinking. I have an idea that will reimagine the Founders and what we're capable of accomplishing together. Let me share my vision with you..."

Seda returned to his ship with the Marines at his back. They went back to the crew quarters, and Seda headed to the bridge, where he found someone he hadn't expected to see sitting in his seat. "Hello, Ranger."

"I heard what you said to Anders," the Myrad said.

"You have a bug in his office," Seda said as a matter of fact.

"If what you said is true, I no longer have a place in the Founders."

Seda smiled. "Quite the opposite, in fact. I plan to leverage your unique set of skills even more."

"But you told Mason—"

"What he needed to hear," Seda finished. "He's leaving and won't return for years, and in all likelihood, never."

The assassin cocked his head. "Tell me what your real vision is..."

CHAPTER 23

NEW BEGINNINGS

Tulan Port, Playa

REYNE STRODE INTO THE STATIONHOUSE, past his office, and through the Collective wing. He cringed at the bots still working on the odds and ends in the hallway and sidestepped a spider bot busily working on a light switch, giving it a wide berth. He hustled past other bots to reach Hadley's office and jumped inside.

He found Hadley's assistant organizing files. She looked up when he entered. "Oh, hello Stationmaster. What can I do for you?"

"Do you know when Hadley will be back?"

Melody shook her head. "She won't. She's been replaced."

Reyne leaned a hand on the doorway. "She's gone?"

She thought for a moment. "Yes, but her ship might not have left yet. She was going to take today's transport home."

He spun on his heel and hurried through the hallway, oblivious to the bots this time around. As he walked, he contacted dock control through his wrist comm. "Hey, this is Aramis Reyne. Has the Alluvian transport left yet?"

"*No, but it's in its launch sequence.*"

"Hold it," he said. "I'm on my way to it now."

"*Sure. Do you need security support?*"

"I've got this one."

He went to grab his coat but noticed the tunnel to the dock was now open. He smiled and took off running through it. The tunnel was cold and dark, the surfaces still rough, but the shortcut shaved ten minutes off the outside walk. When he reached the docks, he commandeered a cart and sped to the Collective concourse. It was even colder in there, and he regretted not bringing his coat. Shivering, he drove until he stopped in front of the large transport ship with Collective markings. Its engines were running, sending steam billowing across the walkways. He stood before the ship, connected to Hadley's comm, and sent a message.

MEET ME ON THE DOCK. VERY IMPORTANT.

He hugged himself and shook while he waited. Eventually, the door opened, and Hadley walked down the ramp. She approached Reyne with brows furrowed.

"Hi," he said.

She managed a smile. "Hi." After a moment, she spoke again. "What are you doing here?"

He shrugged, still hugging himself. "We have a date. I plan to take you out to a proper Playan dinner."

She belted out a laugh. "That's why you're here?" She shook her head. "Reyne, that's sweet, but I've lost my job. When I didn't stand up for Simon, evidently that revealed that I'm unbecoming of a Legacy Star executive. I hate it, but we won't be able to work together anymore."

"No problem. I already quit my job."

"What? Why did you do that?"

Reyne made a face. "It wasn't for me."

"So, we're just two people without jobs and standing out in the cold."

He smiled. "Yeah, we make quite the pair, don't you agree?"

She glanced back at the ship before turning back to him. "But I can't stay. I have no job, no money."

"I've been thinking about that resort idea of yours, and I think it's got merit. Though, maybe we start on a smaller scale, more like a bed and breakfast."

She smiled and shivered. "I like the sound of that."

"So you'll stay?"

She nodded. "Yes, I'll stay." Then she held up her hand. "But we're never drinking your tea again. If you want tea, you're coming back to my place."

A smirk climbed Reyne's face. "Your place, huh? I have a sudden hankering for tea."

She laughed again, and he pulled her into his arms. She felt good, and Reyne realized that for the first time in a very long time, he felt pretty damn good, too.

BLACK SHEEP

A new series in the Fringe universe!

An alien ship. Stolen colonists. All Throttle wanted was a vacation. What she got was a new star system filled with danger.

Fifteen years into a twenty-year voyage, Captain Throttle Reyne is looking forward to taking a break from dealing with malfunctions, glitches, and the hassles of monitoring a thousand colonists in cryosleep.

But when her colony ship breaks down in the middle of nowhere, Throttle and her crew must leave the colonists behind to search for help. They find a ship that's not only missing a crew... it's clearly not from their star system.

It's the discovery of a lifetime. All they need to do is tow the mysterious vessel back to their colony ship for further study and Throttle won't ever have to work again. One problem. While they're away, the colony ship is stolen—with the colonists still on board.

Throttle gives chase to a lawless star system on the outer rim. To get their colonists back, they must take on the pirates and gang lords who will do anything—and sell anyone—to make a buck.

They play dirty. But Throttle and her crew play dirtier.

Get your copy today!

THE COLLECTIVE

The Collective was a collection of six terraformed planets in nearby systems within the Milky Way galaxy. After the Fringe War, only Alluvia and Myr remain in the Collective. The remaining four planets left to form the Alliance of Free Colonies.

MYR is a silver-rich, water-rich world with idyllic islands. Myr was the first settled planet in the Collective. Myrads have argyria and take great pride in their blue-hued skin.

ALLUVIA is a water-covered world and home to First City, the Collective's largest city. Alluvia was the second settled planet in the Collective and has the highest gravity of all six worlds. Alluvia has thick cloud cover and frequent storms.

TERRA is a battle-scarred world, where fuel for space travel is drilled. Its fringe station is Rebus Station. As the planet nearest to Alluvia and Myr, Terra played a pivotal role in the Fringe War.

DARIOS is the most naturally habitable world and provides much of the food supply to the six worlds. Its fringe station is Sol Base, which is being rebuilt after being hit by the blight.

SPATE is a desert-like world and has the largest fringe station, Devil Town, known for its massive garden.

PLAYA is the furthest world from Alluvia and Myr. It has low gravity and freezing temperatures. Its fringe station is Tulan Port, built between the ruins of Tulan Base and Ice Port.

SPACE COAST is an asteroid belt that is home to smugglers, pirates, and other outlaws. Its fringe station is Nova Colony, where the infamous Uneven Bar is located.

ABOUT THE AUTHOR

Rachel Aukes is the award-winning author of over thirty novels, including *100 Days in Deadland*, which made Suspense Magazine's Best of the Year list. She is also a Wattpad Star, her stories having over seven million reads. When not writing, she can be found flying old airplanes over the Midwest countryside and catering to an exceptionally spoiled fifty-pound lapdog.

Join Rachel's spam-free newsletter to be the first to hear about new releases: www.rachelaukes.com/join

ACKNOWLEDGEMENTS

With extreme thanks to my editors, Stephanie Riva and Laurel Kriegler, for helping make this story shiny; and to my jack-of-all-trades, Rob Shores, for catching all the little things that could cause really big problems. Thank you to the Early Reader Brigade for giving an untested book a read. And thank you, my readers, for your messages, cheers, and enthusiasm.